LONE STAR HOSTAGE

Delores Fossen

Lone Star Books

Copyright © 2024 Delores Fossen

All rights reserved

The characters and events portrayed in this book are fictitious. Any similarity to real persons, living or dead, is coincidental and not intended by the author.

No part of this book may be reproduced, or stored in a retrieval system, or transmitted in any form or by any means, electronic, mechanical, photocopying, recording, or otherwise, without express written permission of the publisher.

Cover design by: Danielle Ness
ISBN: 978-1-965032-01-5
Library of Congress Control Number: 2018675309
Printed in the United States of America

CHAPTER ONE

———— ☆ ————

Presley Nolan stared at the bloody shirt in the clear plastic evidence bag on his boss' desk. It was a women's size small, sleeveless, and yellow silk. Or rather, it had once been yellow.

Now, the predominate color was rusty red dried blood.

And there was a jagged rip in the fabric near the neckline.

Those were attention-getters, all right. Then again, so was the sticky note attached to the top that had only three words written on it.

From the hostage.

Yeah, *hostage* was a gut-punching word, but coupled with the blood and what appeared to be that knife slash on the fabric, this looked damn bad.

Normally, a kidnapper allowed some time for his or her demands to be met before inflicting any kind of injury or violence. Then again, the violence could have happened during the abduction. In his experience, most hostages fought back and resisted if they could.

"A courier delivered the top about forty-five minutes ago," his boss, Ruby Maverick, explained.

Presley yanked his attention from the top and toward Ruby. "Delivered it here at headquarters?" he asked.

Ruby, who commanded a room just by walking into it, or breathing, nodded.

"Ballsy," he grumbled.

Maverick Ops was *the* elite security team in central Texas, and it was indeed a bold move for a kidnapper to drop off something like that right on their doorstep.

Or rather hire someone to do it.

"A courier brought it?" Presley guessed.

"Yes, and while the cops are still interviewing him, he doesn't appear to have any connection to the hostage, Victoria Wessington. Report on screen," Ruby ordered her AI app that controlled all the tech bells and whistles in her office.

A blonde-haired woman's image popped onto the wall monitor. Victoria Wessington, no doubt.

"Approximately four hours ago at eight AM, Mrs. Wessington was abducted from the parking lot of her downtown office in San Antonio," Ruby explained. "She runs two foundations and was the only one in the private parking lot at the time. According to her assistant, she'd gone in early to catch up on some work. That was her routine for a Monday morning."

So, the kidnappers would have known she would likely be there. Later, Presley would want to know the names of anyone aware of Mrs. Wessington's routine or schedule, but he held back questions and let Ruby continue with the briefing.

"The security and nearby traffic cams were jammed," Ruby informed him, "but according to an eyewitness who was across the street, two men wearing balaclavas dragged Mrs. Wessington from her office and threw her into a black van. The witness didn't get the license plate number but did call the police. By the time they arrived, the van was nowhere in sight."

When Ruby finished, Victoria Wessington's background info began to scroll across the monitor beneath her photo.

"Aged fifty-two, no criminal record," he read aloud. "No bio offspring but the stepmother of two adult kids. Married for twenty-eight years to..." Presley stopped because he suddenly saw the reason for the kidnapping. "Jesep Wessington, aged sixty-nine, real estate mogul and owner of Wessington Diamonds."

Ruby made a sound of agreement. "He's reported to be worth about fifty million, along with being the main supplier of diamonds to the state. Victoria has her own wealth though, since she's the sole heir to her late parents' global export business."

"Yeah, that'll do it." Those were a lot of reasons for a kidnapper to target the woman.

But it didn't explain why Ruby had called him in. Or why there were two cops standing at the back of Ruby's office. Ruby had introduced them as Detectives Albert Delaney and Seth Martinez.

Before signing on at Maverick Ops, Presley had done a stint in military special forces and had then been a cop at San Antonio PD, and while these two were vaguely familiar, he didn't personally know them. Nor had Presley questioned them—because after Ruby had made the introductions, the bloody top had snagged his attention.

"This arrived with the blouse," Ruby went on. She motioned toward the sheet of paper beside it that had also been sealed in a San Antonio PD plastic evidence bag.

Unlike the sticky note, there were more than three words, and they were hand scrawled in block letters.

"Victoria Wessington's right index finger will arrive if demands are not met in a timely fashion," Presley read aloud. "After that, who knows what kind of dirty, ugly things will happen to her. My advice? Meet the demands."

"What a cocky piece of shit," Presley muttered, looking at Ruby. "And the demands?"

"That came in the form of a phone call about five minutes after the blouse and letter arrived," Ruby explained.

Judging from the timing, that would have been shortly before Ruby had contacted him and asked him to come to her office right away.

"Jesep Wessington wants me to rescue the hostage?" he came out and asked. "Why me and not the cops?"

"Because the kidnappers demanded you do it," Ruby said.

Well, shit on a stick. That was another gut punch.

Presley shook his head. "I don't know anyone in the Wessington family, so why me?"

"Not just you," Ruby muttered, and she gave a voice command to play the recorded call.

Seconds later, the mechanically altered voice poured through the room. It sounded like something straight out of a cheesy cartoon.

"Presley Nolan and former Lieutenant Billie Cooper will deliver the ransom of the diamonds known as the Marbury collection at a time and location to be specified in the next communication."

"Billie," Presley grumbled.

Now, that was a name he had no trouble recognizing. Once, she'd been his boss at San Antonio PD, but now she worked for Ruby's main competition, Strike Force.

"Hell," he added.

Ruby studied him. "Billie should be here any moment. Do you have a problem working with her?"

"No," he was quick to say.

Did he?

Maybe he did.

Though he damn sure shouldn't. This was the job, and personal crap had to be shoved aside.

But thankfully, Presley didn't voice all the waffling that was now going on in his head about Billie Cooper. They'd certainly worked together before, on a few high-profile cases, but that wasn't what was front and center right now.

It was the last time he'd seen her.

The incident.

Something he'd been trying damn hard to forget.

Now, he was not only going to have to face that incident, but he would also need to figure out why the hell the kidnappers had requested the two of them. That meant going through all those old cases.

And their personal lives.

Going through everything because requesting them could be key to identifying the kidnappers.

Well, maybe.

It was also possible the request was a smokescreen to throw them off a scent. Often situations like this involved family members.

"Where's Mrs. Wessington's husband?" Presley asked. "I'm guessing he knows about this?"

"He knows." That response came from Martinez. "He's opted to stay at his estate on the west side of San Antonio and wait for further instructions."

Presley stared at him. "Is he a suspect?"

"Not at the moment." It was the second cop who answered that time. "But we're looking."

"Yeah, I'll bet you are," Presley muttered.

"What's the Marbury collection of diamonds?" he asked, directing that at Ruby.

She put a picture on the monitor of about a dozen diamonds. "Value is about six million. Wessington doesn't own them. They belong to a group of investors who turned them over to Wessington's people so they could be appraised and then resold."

So, it sounded as if Wessington was simply the middle man on this. Did that mean anything in the grand scheme of this kidnapping? Maybe.

Presley shifted to the cops. "Is Wessington onboard with paying the ransom?"

"Not exactly," Martinez said.

Presley huffed. "Let me guess. He wants to substitute fakes or inferior stones to try to fool the kidnappers?"

Martinez nodded. "Mr. Wessington has expressed his hope that you'll be able to rescue his wife and that handing over the decoy diamonds won't be necessary."

"That's a good hope," Presley said, the sarcasm dripping. "It could get his wife killed."

He might have had a whole bunch to say about that if there hadn't been a knock at the door.

"Come in," Ruby said.

The door opened, and there she was. Billie Cooper. Even though Presley had already steeled himself up to see her, he clearly hadn't done enough in that particular department.

As usual, she got to him.

Billie was a blast from the past. A trip down memory lane and a pain in his ass all rolled into one. Yeah, she got to him all right because even after the shitstorm two years ago, the heat was still there, waiting to strike and send their lives to hell in a fast-moving handbasket.

"Presley," she said, his name seeping out of her mouth along with a stream of breath. Apparently, she hadn't done enough steeling up either.

She was tall, only three inches shorter than his six foot two height, and while she had a wiry build, she also looked tough.

And he knew she could be.

He hadn't seen her in two years, since that shitstorm, and there had been some changes. Her shoulder-length brown hair was now cut in a short, choppy, couldn't care less kind of way that suited more than the polished style of her lieutenant days. It framed that amazing face.

And a black eye.

"I, uh, had a few problems with a noncustodial ex who was trying to take his kids," she muttered when she saw him studying her. She turned to Ruby. "Billie Cooper."

"Ruby Maverick."

She nodded. "My boss speaks well of you."

Ruby smirked. "Yes, I'll bet he does." Apparently, it was the day for sarcasm since Ruby's comment was doused in it. "Your boss has briefed you on what's happening?"

"He did on my drive over. Victoria Wessington

has been kidnapped, and Presley and I are supposed to do the exchange. Why us?" she asked, volleying glances at everyone in the room.

"We don't know yet," Ruby informed her. "But my techs are going through all the cases where Presley and you worked together to see if there are any red flags. I understand that the two of you never worked a kidnapping case together?"

Billie shook her head. "Not directly. We were homicide. The one and only time I recall us getting involved in something like that was when things went south and the hostage was killed."

"Yes, that investigation is being looked at," Ruby assured her.

Presley didn't have to any looking to recall the details. It was the case that had started the shitstorm, and it had ended with a woman dead. And Billie and him in bed for what he supposed was comfort sex.

There hadn't been a whole lot of comforting involved.

And afterward, there'd been a hell of a lot of payback.

Within an hour after she'd left his bed, and him, Billie had resigned from SAPD because, hey, sleeping with a subordinate was an unforgivable no-no in her book. A few weeks later, Presley had turned in his badge as well and had ended up leaving to work for Ruby.

Yeah, indeed a shitstorm.

Billie nodded a greeting to the two cops and

then made her way to the evidence bags on the desk. Presley stepped back to clear the path for her, but he wasn't fast enough. Her arm brushed against his. Just a brush.

He noticed.

So did she.

And while Billie didn't mutter any profanity, he could sure see it in her gray eyes. Eyes that she quickly pinned on the top.

"The blood's been tested?" Billie asked with her attention still on the evidence bag.

"It has been," Ruby verified. "It's Mrs. Wessington's. Her DNA was on file because she was a bone marrow donor a few years back. Do you know any of the Wessingtons?" Ruby asked.

Billie nodded. "I met her stepson, Ari, when he came to Strike Force to have us try to retrieve some stolen merchandise. We didn't take the assignment though because…" She stopped, her mouth tightening as if she'd just tasted something very sour. "Because Ari said he preferred to have a man on the job."

The two women exchanged a *heard that before* look.

"My boss turned down the request and advised Ari to go elsewhere," Billie tacked onto that.

Presley didn't personally know her boss, Owen Striker, but the guy just went up a couple of notches in his book.

So, Ari Wessington had a problem with women. Did that include his stepmother? Again, that was something Presley would need to find out.

The landline on Ruby's desk rang, the sound shooting through the room. "It's the kidnappers," she said, glancing at the screen where Unknown Caller was displayed. She gave the verbal command to record the call, and she put it on speaker before she answered.

Once again, Presley heard the same mechanical voice from the previous call. "It's showtime," the cocky asshole said.

"We require proof of life before any exchange is made," Ruby interjected.

"Yes, I figured you'd want that. Scream for them, sweetheart."

It didn't take long. Seconds. Before Presley heard the shriek of what he was pretty sure was fueled by pain. It echoed through the room, and happened just as Ruby got a text.

Ruby muttered something he didn't catch and ordered the photo she'd just gotten on the monitor. Even though the woman was gagged, her face bloodied and bruised, and her hair a tangled mess, Presley could see enough of the hostage's features.

This was indeed Victoria.

Alive.

But nowhere near well.

The photo would be examined for any clues as to her location, but with what appeared to be a white sheet as a backdrop, Presley wasn't holding out much hope for that.

"Mrs. Wessington is obviously having a bad day," the kidnapper joked. "Come and get 'er, and don't forget to come alone, just the two of you, and bring the goodies. Bring them to the Sanderson family park."

"Sonofabitch," Presley grumbled under his breath while Billie muttered a "Damn it."

It was a sunny, warm October day, and that park would no doubt be jammed with families and kids. Added to that, it was in the city center, a good twenty minutes from where they were now, and they'd have to pick up the fake diamonds first. Along with working out a plan to keep bystanders from getting caught up in this.

"Presley and Billie," the voice continued. "Tread carefully. Wouldn't want another hostage dying on your watch, would you?"

Billie and he repeated their profanity and exchanged a look. No words passed between them, but Presley knew what she had to be thinking; this was somehow linked to that last case they'd worked together.

"Try to keep everybody alive this time," the voice taunted.

The tone had changed. It was still that cartoony crap, but Presley heard the dangerous edge to it. Then, he heard the next to impossible condition for Billie and him to save Victoria Wessington.

"You've got thirty minutes," the voice said. "Get here by then, or bring a trash bag to pick up the bloody pieces of her."

And the woman screamed in agony again as the call ended.

———— ☆ ————

CHAPTER TWO

---- ☆ ----

Victoria's scream was still echoing through Billie's mind as Presley and she drove toward the park. He was going at a bat out of hell speed while Ruby blurted out info through the SUV.

Adrenaline was sky high and pulses were racing.

But that scream was cutting through Billie's focus.

Because she'd heard a scream like that before. Another time, another place. Another woman.

Tread carefully. Wouldn't want another hostage dying on your watch, would you?

No, she didn't, but for the kidnapper to be able to use that taunt, he or she must have been aware of the case that'd gone horribly wrong. Billie wanted to know how that info had gotten into the kidnapper's hands.

And if it was important in Victoria's abduction.

But for now though, she just tried to shut it all out and listen to Ruby.

"Angel DeLuca will meet you in the parking lot of Merilee's Café, that's a block from the park,"

Ruby spelled out, and her voice sounded a heck of a lot calmer than Billie felt. No need for her to explain who Angel was. He was a former SAPD and now worked for Ruby. "He just picked up the diamonds from Jesep's assistant and is en route to you now."

"The fake diamonds," Presley grumbled like profanity, and that expressed Billie's sentiment.

Hostage extractions were dangerous enough without adding a bogus ransom to the mix. But they weren't calling the shots here. Jesep was, and apparently he valued the diamonds more than his wife's life.

"Yes," Ruby muttered, her disproval there as well. "Once Angel has handed off the diamonds to you, he'll head to the park and set up surveillance while staying out of sight. I've also just gotten approval for a drone to go in, and I'll send you the feed once I have it."

Good. The drone could help them pinpoint Victoria's location. Hopefully, anyway. Billie doubted the kidnappers would have her out in the open, not unless they had a way to protect themselves. They would no doubt know the cops could and would use SWAT snipers in situations like this.

"How many cops will be nearby?" Presley asked, barreling down the interstate toward their exit.

"Four plain clothes," Ruby provided. "I'm vetting them now. Judging from the initial search, the two of you never worked with any of them."

Not surprising. SAPD had over 2500 cops on duty, and probably at least a couple of hundred of them would have joined the force or transferred in after Presley and she left two years ago.

"What's your ETA?" Ruby asked.

"Ten minutes," Presley relayed.

"Good. That should give you time to park and get your bearings. Keep your earbuds open at all times so I can hear what's going on. Angel will give me a visual of you. Vest up," she tacked onto that.

They'd already put in the buds and donned vests before Presley had sped away from Maverick Ops' headquarters. They'd covered the vests with shirts to conceal both them and their shoulder holsters. Presley had had such a shirt in his SUV, and Billie had gotten one of her own from her go-bag.

"Message me after you've left Angel," Ruby instructed. It sounded as if she was on the verge of hanging up, but that didn't happen. She paused. "I'll be looking into that case the kidnapper mentioned. The one where a female hostage died. Anything I should know about it?"

"Other than I failed?" Presley said. The dread was there in his voice. In his intense brown eyes, too.

"*I* failed," Billie was quick to interject. "I was the senior officer on that investigation."

"Yes, other than that, tell me what happened," Ruby responded in a matter of fact tone.

Presley launched into the explanation. "Two years ago, Helana Frankfort killed her married lover, Charlie Belmont, after a heated argument. Charlie was friends with our captain, so he pressured Billie to lead the investigation. She tapped me as her partner, and we were a couple of hours into it when we learned that Helana had taken Charlie's wife, Sandy, at gunpoint."

He stopped to gather his breath, and Billie took up the recap.

"We got a tip where Helana might be holding Sandy, and since it was close to where we were, Presley and I went in pursuit." Again, Billie had to fight back those memories that were merging with the sound of Victoria's scream. "When we arrived at the location, we saw the women were outside a motel room, and there was a struggle in process. Sandy was trying to escape. Helana was armed. We didn't have a clean shot so we attempted a negotiation."

"It failed," Presley finished. "And Helana killed Sandy while she was screaming for us to save her."

"Helana is dead or in jail?" Ruby questioned.

"The latter," Presley supplied. "Once she'd killed Sandy, she tried to turn the gun on herself, but we stopped her. She was convicted and received two consecutive life sentences."

Ruby stayed quiet for a moment. "I'll look into anyone connected to that case. Anyone who might have a grudge against the two of you."

"You think Presley and I could be the reason

Victoria was taken?" Billie came out and asked.

"It could be playing into it," Ruby replied. "But millions of dollars' worth of diamonds could be, too."

True. Money was a huge motive. But revenge could be as well, and Presley and she had been dragged into this by the kidnappers requesting them. So, Billie made a mental note to do her own digging into Sandy's murder.

"Keep me posted," Ruby added a moment later, and this time, she did end the call.

Presley took the exit, and the logjam of traffic ahead of them caused him both to curse and slow down. Even though he no longer lived in San Antonio, he obviously remembered his way around the back streets of the city because he took one.

"If there's a connection between Sandy and this, we'll find it," he muttered. Obviously, they were on the same wavelength, and it sickened her to think there was a possibility that Victoria had been snatched in some vendetta. "But the connection might be that the kidnappers could believe we're screw-ups, that we won't pose a threat to them getting the diamonds."

Billie hadn't considered it from that angle, but Presley was right. They, and therefore SAPD, had received a lot of bad press about it, partly because someone had recorded Sandy being murdered on their phone and uploaded it to social media. It'd gotten thousands of hits before the cops had managed to get it taken down.

"All that's for later," he muttered. "Right now, we deal with getting back the hostage."

Billie fixed that in her mind. They couldn't save Sandy, but they stood a chance of rescuing Victoria.

Presley threaded his way through the streets, and when they reached the diner, she immediately saw Angel in the parking lot. He'd worked mainly deep cover when he'd been on the job, but she had seen him often enough with Presley to know who he was. And now, like Presley and their other former cop friend, Jace Malley, they were all security specialists at Maverick Ops.

Angel moved to the SUV the moment Presley stopped and lowered the window. He nodded a greeting to both of them before he handed Presley a small black cloth bag.

"Let's hope the fakes are good," Angel muttered. "Be safe," he added, stepping away so that they could drive off.

Presley handed her the bag, and she shoved it into the front pocket of her jeans. It was mind-blowing to think that something so small could be worth so much. Well, they would be if these were the real deal.

While Presley drove the few blocks to the park, Billie checked her primary weapon and the small snub-nosed backup piece that she carried in a slide holster at the back of her jeans. Both were ready. So was she. Now, she had to pray that all went well.

Presley pulled to a stop in the parking lot, and even though they'd expected it to be jammed, both of them muttered some profanity as they looked out at the sea of people. She scanned the crowd, looking for anyone and anything that didn't fit. She knew Presley was doing the same thing.

"Nothing stands out," he muttered.

She had to make a sound of agreement. Then again, she seriously doubted the kidnappers would have a bloody, battered woman in this mix. So, where the heck were they? The question had barely had time to register in her mind when she heard Ruby's voice through the earbud.

"Incoming drone feed," Ruby let them know.

The footage immediately popped onto the dash monitor. It was grainy but detailed enough for her to see their SUV. And Angel's van as it drove past them toward the other end of the parking lot. Once he was in place, he might have a better view than they did.

"Feed is being analyzed. So far, no sign of Victoria," Ruby added.

The seconds crawled by, and the waiting fueled both her worry and the adrenaline. Angel's text didn't help with that, either.

"Nothing," he messaged.

Since there wasn't anything else for her to do, Billie scanned the crowd again, slower this time, and she spotted what she thought might be one of the plain-clothes cops. She was so focused on her search that when the ringing sound of her phone shot through the SUV, it caused her to gasp.

Billie frowned when she looked at the screen. "Unknown Caller."

"One of the kidnappers," Ruby supplied. "I didn't give them either of your contact info."

So, they were resourceful since only a handful of people had her number. That didn't help with the knot already in Billie's stomach.

"Trace and recording activated," Ruby said a moment later. "Take the call on speaker."

Billie did, and she didn't have to wait long before she heard that irritating fake voice. "I see you followed instructions. Good job. No one's died on your watch today. Not yet, anyway. Let's keep it that way."

"We're here at the park," Billie stated. "Where are you?"

"Not at the park." He laughed as if that were a hilarious joke. "I'm, uh, elsewhere with the lovely Victoria. Here's what you need to do to get her back. Come to 637 Barlett Street on the south side of the city."

From the corner of her eye, she saw Presley's shoulders snap back. They turned toward each other, their gazes colliding, and Billie knew something was wrong. Really, really wrong.

"Probably no need to put that address in the GPS," the kidnapper added. "Because Presley will know the way. Hope it doesn't bring back too many bad memories for you." The jerk laughed. "Be there in fifteen minutes, or you know the drill—cut off body parts."

The second he hung up, Billie blurted, "What's going on? How do you know that address?"

A muscle tightened in his jaw. "It was my childhood home until I was ten." Presley threw the SUV into reverse and backed out of the parking lot. "And it's the house where my father murdered my mother."

CHAPTER THREE

———— ☆ ————

"Shit," Presley muttered. "Shit, shit, shit."

And he kept saying it while he tried to tamp down this mental firestorm. Images and memories of one of the worst days of his life.

Yeah, this was not going to be fun.

"I didn't know that about you," Billie said, her voice making it through the loud buzz in his head.

"A lot of people don't know," he settled for saying.

Ruby did though, but while she could no doubt hear every word of this conversation, she was staying quiet about it. Probably because she knew what was most important right now was mapping out the new location. Or working out the possible kinks. Maybe, too, figuring out what the hell to do with an operative who might be falling apart.

But Presley wouldn't do that.

Not with a life at stake.

A personal crisis would just have to wait. He would suck it up and deal, and he kept mentally repeating that as he drove toward a house that he'd vowed never to see again.

"Two plain-clothes cops are heading to the address now," Ruby finally spoke up. "Angel will get there as fast as he can. I'm pulling up a street view and information about the house, but, Presley, tell me about it. About the interior, about the neighborhood. Where is a hostage likely to be stashed here?"

He needed a couple of breaths first and to do a hard shake of his head to clear it. He even bashed his fist on the steering wheel. Then, he answered her while dragging himself right back to that pit of hell.

"One-story brick in what was once a middle-class neighborhood that I've heard has gone straight downhill over the years." He kept his tone as if this was a routine briefing. "Three bedrooms, two baths. Eleven windows," he added, doing a quick mental count, "and two doors. The backdoor feeds into a large yard with a greenbelt behind it."

Which meant unless things had changed, there were no neighbors to see what the heck was going on.

"My guess is the kidnappers would hold Victoria in the bedroom at the far back of the house. That's on the right as you face it," he added as he drove. He didn't glance at Billie. Couldn't. He didn't want her to see the emotion that he knew would be in his eyes. "There's only one window in that room, and it faces the side yard where there used to be a high fence."

It'd been his room.

And also where he'd found his mother dead.

That'd happened when he had come home from school. Seconds later, Presley had found his dad, dead from a self-inflicted gunshot wound to the head, in the main bedroom on the other side of the house. Presley had no idea what his mother had been doing in his room, and since she was dead, it was one of those mysteries that would never be solved.

What wasn't a mystery was that the kidnappers had known this had once been his home. They knew what had happened there.

Hope it doesn't bring back too many bad memories for you.

So, yeah, this was connected to him.

"The kidnappers could be using this location to rattle you," Ruby commented a moment later. "That might be all there is to it. That, and the fact that the house has been vacant for two years now. So are the houses on either side of it."

That could definitely play into a kidnapper's plan, having the house and the surrounding area to themselves. But Presley thought it was more than that.

But what was the *more*?

He didn't know. Yet.

"What's your ETA?" Ruby asked, cutting off any possible answers that Presley might have to his own questions. Those answers were best saved for later, anyway.

Focus.

"We'll be there in ten to fifteen minutes, depending on traffic," he answered. Which meant the kidnappers hadn't given them much time. Still, if they could get the two cops and Angel in place, that would be enough backup.

Hopefully.

"I'll get the drone there," Ruby added and ended the call.

Presley kept on driving, kept on moving through the syrupy downtown traffic. Since Billie was in on this potential shitstorm with him, Presley knew he had to tell her something. So, he picked the most sanitized version he could think of.

"As a newborn, I was abandoned at a fire station. I was adopted by a seemingly normal couple, Jeanie and Hugh Nolan. I was raised here, in this house where we're going. It wasn't a perfect life, but it was solid enough. I never went hungry, and there was no abuse."

"So, what went wrong?" Billie asked when he fell silent.

Presley knew this because he'd looked at the police file once he'd become a cop. "My mom had asked my dad for a divorce. According to some of her friends, she'd met someone else. My dad went ballistic when she told him, and he shot and killed her. Then, he went to his bedroom, wrote a note to me saying he was sorry, and he went out with a single shot to the head." He stopped. Had to. "After that, CPS took over and I was put in a foster home."

Billie no doubt knew about him ending up in the system. It'd been a good home, for the most part, but it'd recently been in the news for an old murder that'd happened there.

"Ruby could be right," Billie concluded. "The kidnappers could have chosen this spot because they knew it would be an emotional gut punch. It could throw you off your game and make you a less formidable opponent."

"Maybe, he admitted. "But if they wanted less formidable, why not demand someone other than the two of us do the drop? Why not pick Jesep or his two likely pampered trust fund kids?"

"Because one of them could have orchestrated this and be paying the kidnappers," Billie was quick to point out.

It was something that had already occurred to him. Still, why choose someone who could kick the kidnappers' asses? Yeah. That didn't make sense.

Shoving that aside as well, Presley took the turn on Barlett Street and glanced around to make sure they weren't about to be attacked. He didn't see any threats, but he'd heard right about the neighborhood going downhill.

Hell on steroids, this was bad.

He drove past house after house in serious disrepair. Yards, too, with weeds waist high in places. Abandoned graffiti junkers lined the streets, and he imagined it would be easy to stash a hostage in one of those cars and then lay in wait inside the house.

"This feels wrong," Billie remarked, obviously picking up on the bad vibe, too.

Presley made a sound of agreement and parked just up the street from the house. It was just as rundown as the rest of the neighborhood, but all the windows looked intact.

"Drone feed isn't showing anyone around the residence," Ruby relayed. "Are the cops and Angel there yet?"

He was about to say no, but then he spotted Angel's van stopping about a half block away. While Angel was parking behind a junker, a black sedan pulled into a spot on the other side of the street. The sedan was about as nondescript as a vehicle could get, which meant these were almost certainly the cops.

"They've arrived," Presley informed Ruby.

"Good. How do you plan to approach the house?"

Presley glanced around. "Well, if the kidnappers are here, then they know we're here as well. And considering this whole deal feels like some kind of sick game, I'm banking on them not gunning us down before we get inside the house. Why end the game that way?"

"Because the goal might be to kill both of you," Ruby pointed out, but then she sighed. "Angel, get in that backyard. Do it quietly and stay out of sight. Once you're in place, Presley and Billie can move in."

Angel didn't waste any time exiting his van,

but he didn't walk directly to the house. He darted into the side yard of a place about four lots up. Presley figured he was heading for the greenbelt. Once he reached the house, he could climb over the fence.

Hopefully undetected.

After all, the kidnappers might carry through on their threat to cut off parts of the hostage if Presley and Billie weren't alone.

Presley gave Angel a few minutes before he gave Billie the nod. They got out of the SUV, and after slipping their hands over their weapons, they made their way to the door. He tested the knob.

Unlocked.

So he opened it and glanced inside.

Thankfully, there was nothing the same about the living room. The pale yellow walls were now a bright green, and it wasn't a fresh job. It was peeling in places as was the popcorn ceiling. The house smelled of rot and dust and death.

He glanced down at the floor. No signs of footprints, but it looked as if someone had recently dragged a broom through it. Maybe to obscure the fact that someone had been here.

"Mrs. Wessington?" he called out.

No response. Not a human one anyway, but he heard some kind of rustling sound. And, yep, it was coming from his old bedroom.

"Angel says the windows are open on the back and sides of the house," Ruby informed them.

So, maybe the noise had been the wind. But

someone had opened those windows. Of course, they could have been that way for a long time since the place was vacant. Hell, squatters could be here.

Billie and he drew their guns and started moving, both of them scanning the area for any traps or anything that could get them killed. But Presley saw nothing other than some roaches as they made their way down the short hall where there were two bedrooms and a bath. His mom had used the other room as an office for her bookkeeping business.

The door to his room was ajar, and Presley peered through the narrow opening. But there was nothing to see but an empty room.

Using his elbow, he opened the door the rest of the way, and the uneven foundation caused it to keep moving and bump against the wall.

And then Presley saw it.

Straight ahead on the wall where his bed had once been. Someone had used a black marker to scrawl TTYS.

"Talk to you soon," he grumbled.

That was not what he wanted from these asshole kidnappers. Nor did he want to see what was on the floor.

Not Victoria Wessington. Not a person at all. But in the center of the room was a small clear glass jar.

And in the jar was the bloody tip of a finger.

———————— ☆ ————————

CHAPTER FOUR

———— ☆ ————

Billie kept quiet as he drove toward Jesep Wessington's downtown office. The cops would be going there as well to give Jesep an update on the kidnapping.

A really bad update.

In a nutshell, his wife hadn't been at the drop location. And it was her finger they'd found. Thankfully, the lab had been able to confirm that right away, but now they'd have to tell Jesep that Victoria had not only been mutilated but that there'd been no indications as to where she was or if she was still alive.

Other than that flippant *TTYS*, the kidnappers hadn't left a note with the grisly jar. Nor had they contacted Presley, the cops or her in the half hour they'd all waited at the house for further instructions.

There was an outside chance that the kidnappers had been in touch with Jesep, but if so, the man certainly hadn't shared that development with SAPD or Maverick Ops.

Judging from the map on the dash, they'd be at

Jesep's office in less than fifteen minutes. Hardly enough time for Billie to try to determine if Presley was up to this visit or if being in his childhood home, AKA the murder house, had shaken his very foundation. It had certainly shaken her to see him like this since Presley had always been rock solid.

It was time to try to pull him out of it.

"Why don't we have a good air clearing?" Billie threw out there.

Presley glanced at her, scowled. But even with that surly expression, she couldn't help but notice he was still one of the hottest guys she'd ever seen. Once, he'd told her that his parents had named him after Elvis because of his black hair, sleepy eyes, and olive skin. And he did indeed have that rock star vibe about him.

"The air doesn't need clearing," he grumbled. "I'm fine. You're fine. We're all fine except for Victoria." He muttered some profanity. "These dicks are playing games with us. With her."

So, that's what was bothering him and not the trip down hell lane. Billie understood his anger and frustration. The kidnappers were indeed playing games, and they'd hurt a woman that they seemingly had no reason to hurt.

Well, unless they knew some insider info.

"The kidnappers could know the diamonds are fakes," she suggested. This wasn't the air clearing she'd anticipated, but it would do. Get him focused back on the assignment.

"Yeah, I considered that. Which points to

someone in the family," he said, stating what she thought as well. "Before I started the drive here, I texted Ruby and requested she find out the terms of Jesep's and Victoria's wills. Whoever has the most to gain might be pulling the strings."

So true.

She hadn't known about his text to Ruby. After discovering the jar, there'd been a flurry of communications. Some through their earbuds, others via text. Jesep's and Victoria's wills were a good angle for them to explore, and while most wills weren't made public, maybe Ruby could find something.

"You want an air clearing about us?" he came out and asked.

Billie did a mental doubletake. No, she didn't especially want to get into the personal stuff, but if it helped with the focus, she'd bite.

"Sure," she said, and was about to add something about where to start.

Presley took care of the starting though. "You certainly dumped me fast after you left my bed."

Okay. They were going *there*. "I did that because I was your boss, and sleeping with you was wrong."

"So you said," he grumbled, and she heard the serious disapproval about that in his voice.

The hurt maybe, too. Well, she'd been hurt, too, because it hadn't been easy to walk away from Presley or her badge.

"I said it was wrong because it was true," she

argued. "You could have reported me."

"For what? An orgasm?" he fired back.

She wasn't sure all of this intensity was for their past. It was likely just being rolled into the stew pot with all the other crap going on.

"I'd never done anything like that before. And it was a mistake," Billie repeated.

"Yeah, got that. You resigned shortly thereafter," he grumbled.

"I should have been fired," she muttered.

"Oh, please." He stretched out that last word some. "I wasn't some helpless dick that you coaxed into bed."

Billie stared at him. And then did something totally inappropriate. She laughed. Really, really laughed.

"Well, your dick was involved," she said, figuring a light-hearted touch wasn't the way to go. Still, she hadn't been able to stop herself.

She waited for his reaction. And waited. And waited.

Finally, he groaned. "Sorry. I was picking a fight with you because I keep seeing my mother's blood on that floor. And now, I have the new memories of a severed finger. Give me a greedy assed, focused on the ransom kidnapper any day over sonofabitches like these."

She couldn't agree fast enough, and she touched her fingers to the still sore area around her eye. "And give me a sonofabitch with a slower right hook."

He glanced at her, and his face—that incredible face—wasn't sporting nearly as much tension as it had seconds earlier. Or rather, he was sporting a different kind of tension. It seemed to disgust him to see that bruise.

"I hope you kicked his balls into his throat for doing that to you," Presley said.

"That's pretty much what happened. The steel toe of my boot in his family jewels, and he deflated like a balloon."

He stayed quiet a moment. "You mentioned it was a noncustodial abduction. Is the kid all right?"

"Kids. A girl, five, and a boy, seven. Thankfully, they didn't witness the ball-busting. He'd stashed them in a motel room. I took him down when he came out to his car to get some things."

"Good. It's bad when the kids see too much."

The voice of experience. Presley had indeed seen way too much when he'd found his dead parents. She suspected that hadn't been his one and only time either. Not with his stints as a cop and military special forces. Maybe fate would give him a break. A break, too, for Victoria, and they wouldn't end up finding her dead.

"Since you're a stickler for rules, how the hell did you end up working for Strike Force?" Presley asked as he took the final turn toward Jesep's office.

Ah, she'd been expecting something along those lines. Her boss, Owen Striker, had a reputation for toeing the line when it came to the law. Actually, a reputation for occasionally going over the line in some hard situations.

"When I interviewed for the job, I told Owen upfront that I wouldn't break the law," she said. "And I haven't."

She might have added more, but he pulled to a stop in front of the Wessington building. No mistaking it for something else since the name was right there, emblazoned in shiny silver across the front of the limestone building. It looked expensive and lavish, exactly as she'd expected.

Presley parked, and while keeping watch around them, they went inside to an equally impressive lobby. The receptionist, a twenty-something-year-old curvy blonde, gave them a look as if they'd tracked in something smelly and disgusting on their shoes.

"Presley Nolan and Billie Cooper to see Mr. Wessington," Presley said, and they both produced their IDs.

The receptionist took the IDs, studied them, and gave them that look again. "Mr. Wessington is expecting you?"

The question riled Billie because, yeah, he was expecting them, and he should have let his employee know so this part of the visit could be streamlined. Instead, they had to wait for the receptionist to call "up to the top floor." Then, they had to wait—Billie kept watch of the time—for over two minutes before they were allowed into the elevator.

"Either Wessington has bad attention to detail,

or he's fallen apart," Billie guessed.

"Yep, it'll be interesting to see which," Presley agreed.

They rode the elevator to the top floor, and when they stepped off, there was another receptionist, a middle-aged brunette this time. Unlike her downstairs counterpart, this one didn't give them any nasty looks. She ushered them straight into Jesep's office.

Billie glanced around the massive space. Floor to ceiling windows with a view of the San Antonio Riverwalk. Prime real estate. Everything was gleaming and polished, from the marble floors to the wood on the large desk where Jesep was seated.

Jesep was polished, too, with every strand of his silver-white hair in place. Ditto for his dark gray suit. Billie's first impression of him was that he looked like an arrogant jerk. She hoped she was wrong because that kind of personality wouldn't make it easy for them to rescue his wife.

He wasn't alone in the room. There was a woman on the white leather sofa in the seating area that Billie recognized from her photo as Jesep's daughter, Olivia. The man across from her was Ari.

So, the family was all here.

Well, with the exception of Victoria, and even her picture wasn't present in the shiny framed photos on one of the end tables. In that trio of photos was another woman, a much younger Jesep, and Ari and Olivia as children. Billie was guessing this was Jesep's first wife and Ari and Olivia's mother.

"Presley Nolan," he said, and he hiked his thumb to her. "This is Billie Cooper."

"We've met," Ari all but snarled. "You refused the last time I needed help." So, he obviously remembered.

Billie didn't remind him that he was the one who'd done the refusing by not wanting a woman on the case. At least she didn't remind him verbally, but she shot him a cool glance that probably had a tinge of a smirk to it.

"Where's Victoria?" Jesep demanded without introducing himself.

"We don't know," Billie admitted. "Presley and I went to the drop location—"

"Yes, yes, yes," he said impatiently. "The police told me there was a note on the wall and a finger in a jar."

There was no usual look of revulsion when he said that. Not from Ari either. But Billie noted that Olivia turned a little pale. Good. At least someone here was disgusted with what had happened.

"You're both fired for incompetence," Jesep barked. "You should have found Victoria by now and brought her home."

That got Billie's attention back on the man, and before she could say anything, Presley shrugged. "Fine. The kidnappers requested us, so I'll just let the cops know that along with refusing to pay the ransom, you've now put up a roadblock to getting your wife back."

Olivia bolted from the sofa and hurried to her father. "Dad, you can't fire them."

"I can and will," Jesep snapped. "They've failed to do their jobs. They've—"

"No, the kidnappers lied," Olivia corrected. "They're playing around with us, maybe building our desperation to have Victoria safely returned home. And we do want her back," Olivia stated, directing that at Presley and Billie.

"They're not even sure if the blood and that finger is Victoria's," Jesep spat out.

"It's hers," Billie verified. "Your wife's DNA was in the bone marrow registry."

Olivia dragged in a breath, nodded. "Because she donated marrow when I was eight." She paused. "My father and Victoria got close after that."

That reminder seemed to cause Jesep to throttle back some. "I'd been a widower for six years by then," he rattled off as if to explain that he hadn't jumped straight from one wife to another.

But Billie had to wonder if Jesep's gratitude for Victoria saving his daughter's life had played into them getting married. She was certainly having a hard time figuring out why anyone would have wed Jesep. Then again, she didn't know anything but background facts about Victoria. Maybe Jesep and Victoria were a perfect match.

"So, the finger is Victoria's," Ari said, clearly directing his comment to Presley and not Billie.

"What's next? Why haven't the kidnappers been in touch?"

Those were both good questions, and there didn't seem to be any hidden subtext in that. Unlike his father, Ari didn't appear to be blaming Presley and her for what had happened. But that talking man-to-man crap must have riled Presley because he motioned for Billie to dole out the response.

"There could be several reasons why the kidnappers haven't contacted us," Billie replied. "One is building the desperation that your sister mentioned. They could be hoping to capitalize on that and either make a higher or faster demand."

Ari nodded, sparing Billie a glance. "Give us the diamonds now or we cut off more fingers?"

"That's a possibility," Billie confirmed. "But something could have gone wrong with the drop. Maybe the kidnappers thought they were about to be captured and fled to set up another venue for the exchange."

"Bullshit guesses," Jesep snarled. "You don't know what happened to my wife. She could be dead for all you know."

Presley gave the man that look. The one Billie had seen him use when interrogating the worst of criminals. It was a flat-eyed, quit pissing me off glare. And it was very effective.

"Yes, she could be dead," Presley said, his voice low and with a dangerously calm edge. "The kidnappers could have learned the diamonds were fake and killed us. Whose idea was it to try to con people who had total and complete control over Victoria's life?"

Silence fell on the room, and Billie didn't need the answer verbalized. She could tell just by the way Ari and Olivia had their gazes fixed on their father.

"Those diamonds aren't mine to give away," Jesep spat out.

"And you couldn't purchase them for your wife's ransom?" Presley was quick to ask.

The muscles in Jesep's jaw went to war with each other. "No." That was it. He didn't add any further explanation as to why a man of his estimated wealth couldn't shell out money to give his wife a fighting chance of being returned alive.

And in one piece.

"Have the cops taken DNA and fingerprints from you?" Presley asked, keeping his attention pinned to Jesep.

Oh, that didn't set well with the man. "Why would they?" Jesep snarled.

Presley shrugged. "They normally do in situations like this. It's to exclude family members' DNA or prints from any evidence they might find. While we're waiting on the kidnapper to contact us, I can have someone from SAPD lab come over and do that."

Jesep snatched up his phone. "I'll talk to my lawyer about that."

Billie had no idea if the man was just doling

out more of his asshole ways or if he had an actual reason why he wouldn't want the cops to have his DNA.

"Ella, get Tate on the line now," he barked.

"Tate Harrington, his lawyer," Olivia supplied.

Judging from the stink-eye Jesep was aiming at Presley and her, he seemed to believe the call would intimidate them.

Not a chance.

She turned to Presley to see what their next move should be, but before she could say anything, his phone rang. Of course, that amped up the adrenaline because her first thought was this was the kidnapper.

It wasn't.

"It's Ruby," he relayed to her in a whisper, and he motioned for her to follow him out of the office. He didn't answer the call until they were on the other side of the reception area.

"You heard from the kidnappers?" Presley immediately asked when he answered. He didn't put the call on speaker, but Billie moved in close enough so she could hear what his boss had to say.

"No, the lab," Ruby corrected. And she paused a long time. "I don't know what it means yet, but the tech just told me that there's a familial match in the database to Victoria's DNA."

Billie's forehead bunched up because that didn't seem like a big deal. It was probably a relative. That would have occurred to Ruby, too, though. But still, she'd called.

"Who's the match to in the database?" Billie came out and asked.

Ruby blew out an audible breath. "Presley."

———— ☆ ————

CHAPTER FIVE

———— ☆ ————

Presley froze. Just froze. And he couldn't wrap his mind around what Ruby had just said.

Victoria was a familial match to him.

"What the hell?" he muttered, and he started walking. To the elevator. Back down to the bottom floor. Out the door and straight toward his SUV. Billie was right behind him.

"Presley?" Ruby questioned. "Are you still there?"

"Yeah," he managed, and he didn't say anything else until Billie and he were in his vehicle. There, he put the call on the dash speaker, mainly so Billie would hear and be able to make sense of this.

"How close of a familial match?" Billie asked. It was a good question, one that should have occurred to Presley.

"Close," Ruby said, and she continued before Presley could press her for more about that. "She has fifty percent DNA in common with Presley. I've done an extensive background check on Victoria, and there's no indication she's ever had a child."

Finally, it all sank in. And it hit him damn hard.

"I was abandoned at a fire station when I was a newborn. Parents unknown. I could have siblings," he added, quickly doing the math to calculate the age difference between Victoria and him.

Sixteen.

She was sixteen years older than him.

"Or Victoria could be my…" He stopped. Had to. And gathered his breath. "My bio mother."

"Yes," Ruby confirmed. "Social media was barely a blip when you were born thirty-six years ago so there are no public photos to prove that Victoria was ever pregnant. However, she attended a private boarding school in England, and I was able to find out that she left when she was sixteen and returned a year later. I don't have an explanation yet about that gap in time."

Presley was hearing every word Ruby said, but he still wasn't processing it. Victoria Wessington was likely his mother. She'd been kidnapped. And the kidnappers had requested him.

Shit.

They'd requested him!

Presley groaned and hit his fist on the steering wheel. It was all connected. It had to be.

"Take some time to deal with this," Ruby instructed. "I'll call you when I know more. And if the kidnappers contact you, I'll try to negotiate other arrangements for the ransom drop."

"No, don't," Presley managed to say. "I don't want to be excluded from this. Please," he tacked onto that when he realized the snapping tone he'd just used with his boss.

"You're sure?" Ruby asked.

She must have had a lot of faith in him to put the ball in his court on such an emotional, critical matter.

"I'm sure. Keep me in the loop," he insisted.

"Okay," Ruby muttered before she ended the call.

Billie and he sat there in the silence that followed. Thankfully, Billie didn't pepper him with questions or try to comfort him. She just waited, no doubt coming to some of the same conclusions as he was.

"Why would the kidnappers demand you be in on the ransom drop?" he was finally able to ask. "I mean, I get them choosing me now that I know about the familial match. But why you?"

"To create more conflict for you," Billie said without hesitation. "I'm sure there was gossip about us when we both left the force. Maybe even gossip that we'd had a one-off. The kidnappers might have believed they could capitalize on a rift between us by throwing us together."

Okay, Presley could see that, but it didn't answer one huge question. "Why bring us in on this? If this is just about them getting the diamonds, why create conflict? Why not try to make things go as smoothly as possible?"

"Because maybe the endgame isn't the diamonds," she finished for him.

Bingo. And if that was true, then Victoria

hadn't been kidnapped. She'd been *taken.* Of course, that led Presley to another why, and this time, Presley was the one to provide the answer.

"Someone wants Victoria dead," he concluded, "and the kidnapping is a way of covering up her murder."

As he heard the words come out of his mouth, the overwhelming sense of dread tore through him. He'd just learned the possible identity of his birth mother, and she could already be dead.

"I'm sorry," Billie muttered, and she did something that surprised him.

She leaned over and pulled him into her arms. Presley hadn't even known he wanted, or needed, that hug until Billie pressed closer to him and held on.

He held on, too, putting his arms around her and adjusting so their faces were touching. Presley took in her scent. Took in the feel of her. And he got a whole bunch of memories that he shouldn't be getting.

Of that night she'd ended up in his bed.

An incredible ending to a shitstorm of an assignment. Billie had been the only bright spot in that ordeal.

However, it wasn't the first time he'd been attracted to her. No, that had happened right from the start. He'd felt the heat, the lust, the pull from the moment he'd met her. Only her rank and position had kept him from asking her out, and even those barriers had dissolved when they had sex.

The memories kept coming, and Presley felt himself ease back just a little. Just enough for him to brush his mouth over hers. It was a mistake, and he braced himself for her to jolt away. Or, hell, even slap him.

She didn't do either of those things.

Billie made a soft sound. A hitch of breath combined with a moan, and for just a moment, she sank into the kiss. She gave as good as she got. Then, she moved away from him.

There was confusion in her eyes, and what she muttered was pure profanity. He got that. She didn't want this heat. Neither did he. But he was clueless as to how to make it go away, especially since that scorching kiss had seemed to clear some of the cobwebs in his head.

"We need to find Victoria," he stated.

"Yes, we do," Billie stated right back, the determination in both her voice and expression. "Let's go to my house so we'll have some computers to work on. We need to access traffic cams to and from the house on Barlett Street. That and the parking lot of Victoria's office are the only two places that we know for certain that the kidnappers or someone working for them has been."

"True." He pointed to the dash. "Put your address in the GPS."

Billie immediately started doing that just as a report came in from Ruby. It was marked as

Nonurgent with an additional note of: *Deal with what you're going through. I'll handle anything on this if needed.*

As far as he was concerned, everything was urgent at this point. And that meant he wanted to know what was in it.

"Read it to me as I drive," Presley instructed, and he headed to her place on the north side of the city. According to the GPS, it would take them twelve minutes to get there.

"It's a report on Sandy and Charlie Belmont," Billie relayed. "Ruby's looking into it in case that's the reason the kidnappers chose you and me."

Part of him wanted to dismiss the angle, now that he knew about Victoria being his bio-mom. But dismissing it could be a really bad idea. Because Victoria's kidnapping could indeed have been fueled by what had happened to Sandy and Charlie. This entire kidnapping could have been orchestrated to get back at Billie and him and make them pay.

"Helena Frankfort is still in prison for murdering Sandy and Charlie," Billie continued to read. "And she's had no visitors or correspondence to indicate that she's made any moves to try to get revenge for us arresting her."

That was good to have Helena ruled out. The woman was a vicious snake with the heart of a killer. But there was someone else out there who might be playing the revenge card. And that person wouldn't have to do that from behind bars in a maximum security prison.

"What about Sandy's sister, Hattie Sinclair?" Presley asked when he spotted her name in the report.

Billie took a moment, reading the entry. "Two weeks ago, Hattie took a leave of absence from her job as a surgical nurse. She told her boss she was going to volunteer at Doctors Without Borders and that she'd be in touch with him when she was ready to come back."

Shit. That sounded like a red flag to him. "Was Ruby able to verify where Hattie is?" he asked.

"No. But Ruby's trying to track her down." Billie kept reading. "Ruby also says that the lab indicates that Victoria's finger wasn't removed with actual surgical precision, but that it wasn't a sloppy job either. So, that doesn't rule out Hattie one way or another."

Presley couldn't allow himself to think of the horrific pain Victoria had gone through during that ordeal. He couldn't think of a lot of things when it came to her, not yet anyway, so he focused on the kidnapping.

"Hattie could have arranged for all of this," he said, talking it through to hear if it made sense as a theory. "She could have hired the kidnappers and dragged us into this so she could try to mentally torture us and then kill us during the ransom drop."

He paused because this is where the logic of the theory fell short.

Way short.

"Why didn't Hattie go through with killing us when we got to the house?" he asked. "She could have stashed herself in the closet and come out with guns blazing when we entered?"

Billie made a sound to indicate she was giving that some thought. "Maybe because she wants to get away with the crime and the diamonds?" But she shook her head. "Or the diamonds might not even matter."

True. If this was all about getting revenge for her sister's murder, then money wasn't going to appeal to Hattie.

"And there's another thing about this that doesn't make sense. How the heck would Hattie have even known that Victoria could possibly be your birth mom?" Billie pressed. "Because I can't buy that you and I and the choice of hostage played no part in this."

Neither could he. Victoria was a key player, just as Billie and he were. But what the hell were they a key for?

"Victoria's DNA was in the bone marrow registry," Presley reminded her. "As a nurse, Hattie might have access to that. Of course, that doesn't explain how Hattie would have made the leap to compare Victoria's DNA to mine."

"Definitely a leap." She paused. "Unless Hattie learned some other way. We need to find out who knows that Victoria might be your mother."

Yeah, they did, and finally Presley had a focus.

Because that could be the critical piece of info to unraveling this and finding Victoria.

His phone rang, the sound shooting through the SUV, and he answered it when he saw Ruby's name on the screen.

"I just found out something about Jesep's will that you both should know," Ruby explained. "A month ago, he had it completely rewritten."

Presley groaned. "Did he cut Victoria out of the will?"

"No. Just the opposite," Ruby corrected. "He's cut out his kids, and he's leaving his entire estate to Victoria."

———— ☆ ————

CHAPTER SIX

--- ☆ ---

Billie sat in her kitchen, reading through some reports and steeling herself up to face Presley once he came down from his shower. Some steeling up was usually required whenever she was around him.

Blasted attraction.

But she figured she needed an extra boost in her resolve since he'd spent the night in her house. A necessity since they'd needed to work on the investigation. But that necessity came with a high price tag attached.

There was an intimacy having him here, and her body and mind just hadn't allowed her to forget that he had been just across the hall from her in the guest room. Some parts of her body and mind had wanted to go to him. To fall right into his arms and experience, well, everything Presley was capable of doling out in the pleasure department.

In other words—a lot.

The sexual pull had given her some amazing dreams. Thankfully though, those dreams and nudges of heat had been tempered with the reality of what Presley and she were facing.

And had faced.

Having the kidnappers demand they do the ransom exchange. Sending them on a wild goose chase to the murder house. Then, the long, miserable wait to learn Victoria's fate.

Along with that waiting, there'd been the bombshells, including the one about Jesep's will. But that one had been a drop in the proverbial bucket compared to yesterday's other shocker.

Presley had been shaken to the core learning that Victoria was his bio-mother. Shaken once again when the lab had triple-checked and confirmed it. DNA didn't lie, but apparently Victoria had by keeping the secret of her motherhood from her son.

Maybe Victoria had done that because she didn't know where to find Presley. And even if she found him, oh, what a scandal it would have caused. The socialite heiress and wife of…an asshole had given birth at sixteen and abandoned her child. So, Victoria might have been afraid of her secret being revealed.

Was that because she'd been bullied by Jesep?

Or was there something rotten or wrong at Victoria's core?

Billie couldn't judge the woman for giving up her child, but she sure as hell could judge her for abandoning Presley. Victoria could have simply told her doctor that she wanted her child to be adopted, and it would have happened. Of course, maybe there was some underlying reason why Victoria hadn't been able to do that.

The thorough background that Ruby had run on Victoria gave them some glimpses as to those possible underlying reasons. From what Billie had read, Victoria's father had been much like Jesep. Rich, arrogant, and with a *my way or the highway* attitude. Billie couldn't see a man like that approving of his sixteen-year-old daughter having a baby.

And that had led Billie and Presley to yet more digging.

On his bio-father.

Because, hey, he could be at the center of this. He could want to get back at Victoria for discarding their child and presumably him as well. What better way to do that than to drag Presley into the ransom drop so there could be sort of a warped family reunion?

But that theory didn't feel right to Billie.

Yes, it had to be considered, but she just couldn't see a bio-dad having things play out this way. After all, Presley was being punished, too, by having the bombshell thrown at him, and to a bio-father, Presley would be innocent in what Victoria had done.

The problem was there was no DNA match for his bio-dad so the man couldn't be definitively ruled out as a suspect. That meant more digging. More questions. And still no answers.

Including no answers about Victoria's

whereabouts.

The kidnappers hadn't contacted them, and while Billie hated to read too much into that, it could mean that Victoria was dead. She had to shove that aside and get that steeling up in place though when she heard the footsteps and Presley came in.

Great.

Even with what had to be minimal sleep and a mountain of stress, the man still managed to look hot. A cross between his namesake rock star and a Greek god.

Yep, he had her hormonal number, all right.

Presley kept his gaze on her as he went to the coffeemaker and poured himself a cup. "You look… interested," he said.

She figured he meant that in a sexual way, and Billie didn't intend to touch it with a ten-foot pole. Apparently, he did though.

He leaned in and kissed her.

It was just a peck and barely qualified as a kiss. It packed a serious punch, and it took more of that steel for her not to move in and take his mouth as if it were hers for the taking. It wasn't.

Was it?

Billie shoved that stupid question away and put her mind back on the work. Once this investigation was done, then she could maybe do a test drive with Presley to see just where this heat could take them.

"Please tell me we have new information that'll

help us," she threw out there. "Help us find Victoria," she added.

That got the rock star expression off his face, and she watched him shift to the tough operative. "Not really. Jesep refused to talk to the cops about his will. Ruby's setting up a meeting for us with Ari and Olivia, and she'll call us as soon as she's got that in place."

The words had no sooner left his mouth when his phone rang, and when he yanked it from his pocket, she saw Ruby's name on the screen.

"Speak of the devil," he muttered, and he took the call.

"You're on speaker," Presley let his boss know. "Give me good news."

"I don't have any about Victoria. Like you, the techs haven't been able to find anything on the traffic cams. My guess is one of the kidnappers sneaked into the house through the greenbelt, left the jar and the message. There's no evidence to prove that Victoria was ever there."

That meshed with what Billie had found as well. Which meant they were at a standstill.

"FYI, neither Jesep nor his kids have given us DNA samples yet," Ruby went on. "Jesep says he's still talking to his lawyer about that."

Billie groaned, and she wondered if Jesep knew that, at best, this made him look uncooperative, and at worst, it made him look like the one who'd orchestrated this kidnapping.

"Yes, I'm not pleased about that either," Ruby

murmured, obviously hearing Billie's groan. "But Ari and Olivia have agreed to see you at Olivia's home in forty-five minutes," she went on, rattling off the address. "So, I'm guessing you need to get moving, and we can finish this conversation as you make the half hour drive."

"We're moving," Presley assured her, setting aside his coffee and taking out his keys. Billie and he went to her garage, where he'd left his SUV. "Considering Jesep's will, Olivia and Ari have strong motives for kidnapping their stepmom. Kill Victoria first, and the will won't matter."

"That's one of my working theories, too," Ruby agreed. "It could be just one of them, or they could be working together." She paused. "You shouldn't say anything about Victoria being your bio-mother."

"Got that," Presley was quick to agree as he entered the address into the GPS and then backed out of the garage. "Because that would make me a target. Of course, I could already be one if Ari or Olivia know."

"Yes," Ruby muttered. "Because they could be planning on you dying during the ransom drop. They could be hoping it'll look like a tragic accident of you trying to do your job. That means they could intend for Billie to be collateral damage."

"True," Billie admitted.

And that went back to the notion that she was meant to be a distraction for Presley, to throw him off his game. If that was it, the kidnapper was certainly pushing some buttons here.

"Of course, if Ari and Olivia aren't the kidnappers, then maybe there's another reason the two of you were tapped for the job," Ruby went on. "And that brings me to something I just found out about Hattie."

Everything inside Billie went still. No way had she ruled out Sandy's sister coming after them for revenge for Sandy's murder.

"Hattie worked with a doctor who once boarded at the same school as Victoria," Ruby explained. "I'm tracking her down to see if she told Hattie anything about Victoria being pregnant."

Now, that would be a connection that Billie hadn't considered. But it could fit. If Hattie had learned that Presley was Victoria's son, she could have orchestrated this payback plot. If that was her endgame, then Victoria would likely be murdered.

As would Presley and her. Once they'd suffered enough, that is.

"I'll get back to you on whatever I learn about Hattie," Ruby continued. "And as soon as you finish talking to Ari and Olivia, let me know what they had to say."

"Will do," Presley assured her. He ended the call and glanced at her. "You can see Hattie as a kidnapper and killer?"

Billie didn't even have to give this any thought. "Yes. She's enraged enough to kill. Maybe she decided to get rich in the process by getting the ransom." She paused. "But Ari and Olivia have just as strong of a motive."

He made a sound of agreement. "And Jesep."

"And him," she verified. "The will could be a way for him to make himself look innocent. He loved his wife enough to leave her everything, so there's no way he could be behind her kidnapping."

That was as far as Billie got before she had to stop.

"That theory runs out of juice when looking for a motive," Billie concluded. "I've uncovered no evidence whatsoever that Jesep is having an affair. No evidence either that Victoria is planning on divorcing him or that there's been a serious rift in the marriage."

"Same," Presley said. "But there's the greed angle. Victoria is rich in her own right."

"Yes, and I'm betting she owns a lot of old family jewelry and such that's a worth not so small a fortune."

Her phone rang, cutting off the rest of her speculation, and she winced when she saw her boss' name on the screen.

"Owen," she answered, debating if she should put the call on speaker. Owen made the decision for her.

"I hope Presley is with you because I'm with someone you'd probably like to talk with," Owen said. "Hattie Sinclair."

"Hattie," Billie repeated, switching the call to speaker. It only took a couple of seconds for her phone to pair with the SUV's Bluetooth.

"Yes," Owen went on. "I tracked her down at her vacation cabin, and she's agreed to speak with you."

"No, I've agreed to give them a piece of my mind," she heard Hattie snarl.

"Well, hopefully that'll involve some talking," Owen remarked with his usual unruffled tone.

"What I'll say is this," Hattie snapped. "Don't drag me into the shit you've created in your lives. The cops called me. The cops," she said, the venom going up a notch. "They wanted to know if I had any part in kidnapping that rich bitch, Victoria Wessington. Then, they asked me about you."

"And what did you tell them?" Billie pressed.

"That you two are worthless pieces of shit who could get that woman killed. Just like you got my sister killed."

Billie had known it wouldn't take long for Hattie to work her way around to Sandy. "I'm sorry for your sister's death," Billie said for the umpteenth time. And it was the God's honest truth. She was sorry, but what'd happened had been a tragic accident.

"Yeah, right," Hattie grumbled. "Why the hell do you care so much about finding this rich woman when you didn't care enough to get to my sister in time to save her?"

Billie looked at Presley, and they both frowned. "Do you know Victoria Wessington?" Presley asked.

"No," Hattie spat out. "And that's what I told the cops. I also told them what I'll repeat to you. Keep me out of the shit going on in your lives. I want nothing to do with the two of you."

Moments later, Owen came back on the line. "I'm taking you off speaker at my end." There was a slight click. "Did you get what you wanted from her?"

"I'm not sure," Billie said. "Does she have an alibi for, well, any of this?"

"No," Owen answered. "The trifecta definitely applies here."

Which meant Hattie had means, motive, and opportunity.

"Are you two okay?" Owen asked.

Billie gathered her breath. "We're on our way to see Victoria's stepkids."

"Yeah, Ruby's been sending me copies of the reports." He paused. "Say hello from me next time you see Ruby."

"I will." Billie ended the call and then wondered about her boss' tone. Not his trademark one. This had some…heat in it?

But she had to be wrong about that. Everything she'd ever heard was that Owen and Ruby despised each other.

"Yeah, I picked up on that, too," Presley said when they exchanged a glance. "Ruby doesn't have a lot to say about him." He paused. "But I remember her once calling your boss the DV whisperer. What's that about?"

Billie gathered her breath. "He handles the domestic violence cases. When there's overwhelming evidence that a woman's being abused and she comes to us for help, Owen takes the op pro bono. If the abuser is male, Owen goads the abuser into a fistfight, lets him land the first couple of punches, and then Owen beats the shit out of him. If necessary, he repeats the process until the abuser is either incapable of more abuse or he moves on."

"That doesn't sound very whisper-y," Presley muttered.

"It's Owen," she settled for saying. "And it's effective."

"And what happens when the abuser is a woman?" he asked.

She looked at him. "Then, Owen sends in me, and I'm the one who goads, and wins, the fight."

Presley whistled. "The man must really hate abusers."

"He does. His daughter was killed by one." And she winced a little, recalling that his mother had been murdered.

She didn't get a chance to mutter an apology though because his phone rang again. Not Ruby this time. Unknown Caller popped onto the screen.

"Elvis, record the incoming call and alert Ruby. That's the name for my AI program," he added to Billie. "I want Ruby to tap into this so she can listen." Then he hit answer.

"Presley, Billie," the cartoon voice greeted.

"Ready for a new, exciting adventure?"

"Where's Victoria?" Presley demanded.

The kidnapper gave a quick reply. "Good. You're eager. Soon you'll get to see her for yourselves. Come to the old bridge over Comanche Creek."

"What's the address?" Presley wanted to know.

"There's not one. You could say this is out in the sticks. Old bridge. Comanche Creek. About two miles from the out in the sticks town of Outlaw Ridge. You've got one hour. Come alone and all that other blah blah."

Billie immediately used her phone to check the location. Owen lived near Outlaw Ridge so if there was time, she'd get insight about the area from him.

"Scream, baby," the cartoon voice instructed.

And Victoria's blood-curdling scream tore through the SUV. From the corner of her eye, Billie saw every muscle in Presley's jaw turn to iron.

"That was your proof of life," the kidnapper said. "So, get here and save the princess. Oh, and more thing. Don't bother bringing the diamonds. They're fake, aren't they? You don't have to answer that," the kidnapper said before they could respond. "Don't bring them. We have a new demand."

"What?" Presley snapped.

"It's an easy peasy one. You and Billie, you're now the ransom." The kidnapper laughed. "We'll exchange Victoria for the two of you."

CHAPTER SEVEN

———— ☆ ————

Well, hell. This was a development that Presley hadn't seen coming.

Though he should have.

After all, the kidnappers had involved Billie and him right from the start so it was obvious they were going to be key players in this. He just hadn't known it was all about them. He was betting Victoria had only been a pawn to draw them out.

But for what?

And why?

He was certain they would soon find out.

Presley did a U-turn, heading to the location the kidnapper had given him, and it didn't surprise him when he got a call from Ruby.

"The call couldn't be traced," she let them know right off. "And I've sent out a drone to the Comanche Creek Bridge. Are you familiar with the area? Is there a reason the kidnappers chose it?"

"Not familiar," Presley said, and Billie echoed the same.

"But it's near where my boss lives," Billie added, and she put the map of the site onto his dash screen.

"Yes," Ruby muttered, the disapproval coating her voice. "Owen might be a part of this. Not as a kidnapper," she was quick to say when Billie made a sharp sound of disagreement. "But if this goes back to Sandy's murder, then the killer could blame Owen and me since you work for us." She paused. "A few minutes ago, I got a text from the kidnapper, ordering me to the ransom drop. I'm on my way."

Presley cursed again. This definitely couldn't be good, and he suspected they'd all be walking into an ambush.

So, what were their options?

They couldn't refuse to go. That would surely get Victoria murdered, especially if that theory about her being a pawn was true.

"Angel is en route to the sight as well," Ruby went on, and in the background, Presley could hear not only the engine of Ruby's vehicle but also the sound of an incoming text. "And apparently so is someone from Strike Force. Hayes Brodie. Billie, do you know him?"

"Yes," she verified. "I guess you could say he's Owen's right-hand man. They served together as Delta Force officers. A little rough around the edges, but I'd trust him with my life."

"Good. Because that's exactly what you'll be doing," Ruby responded. There was another text ding. "We all will be. And if there are any differences between Strike Force and Maverick Ops, that gets put aside now. Understand?"

"Understood," Billie and Presley agreed.

Presley couldn't help but think though that any beef with Strike Force wasn't between the operatives of the groups but rather between the leaders. He didn't know what had caused that and now wasn't the time to find out.

"The kidnapper knew the diamonds were fake," Presley reminded his boss. "That info had to have come from an insider at the family business. What can we do about that?"

"Hold off on your meeting with Olivia and Ari. Warrants are in the works to get phone and financial records from Jesep and them. And from anyone who works closely with them. I've asked for Hattie's records, too, of course. I want to see who they've been communicating with for the past couple of days."

That was a good start, but unless they were idiots or overly cocky, they must have known this could happen. If one of them was the kidnapper, they had probably covered their tracks by using burner phones.

"Owen was just at Hattie's vacation cabin," Billie relayed to Ruby. She was working with the map, moving it to what was essentially a street view. Or rather a road view, anyway.

"Yes, one of those texts you heard was from Owen," Ruby verified. "He left Hattie's place after she spoke with the two of you. In fact, she immediately told him to get out."

So, in other words, Hattie could have been the one to make the latest call from the kidnapper.

"Owen has someone watching Hattie," Ruby went on, "and she hasn't left the cabin. That doesn't mean she's not pulling the strings."

Ruby was right about that. Of all their suspects, Hattie had the strongest motive for wanting Billie, Ruby, Owen, and him dead. But how the hell had the woman learned about the fake diamonds?

A guess, maybe?

Because she had some kind of insight or knowledge from the family?

Either of those could be true, but getting those answers would have to wait since there was a more immediate question that needed answering.

How were Billie and he going to approach this ransom drop?

Presley looked at the dash screen. At the bridge. And at the thick trees that lined both sides of the small creek. There were dozens of places for the kidnappers to hide and lie in wait. He didn't like any of the options he saw, but he was going to treat this as an extraction. A rescue.

Hopefully, this time, a woman wouldn't be murdered before they could get to her and stop it.

"I think our best bet is for Billie and me to park about a quarter of a mile up from the bridge," he explained to Ruby. "Not in that small clearing just off the road. Too obvious. They'd expect us to park there." He tapped the spot on the map. "But right before that, where there's a rock pile."

It was out in the open. A serious downside for Billie and him having cover, but the upside was that the kidnappers couldn't lie in wait. What they could do, however, was climb one of the nearby trees and shoot them with a rifle.

Presley silently cursed having Billie walk into something like that. But then he reminded himself that she was in the same line of work as he was. She knew the risks. Knew how to take out the enemy, too.

"We can leave the SUV there by that rock pile and get down into the ditch," he continued. "From there, we can make our way to the drop sight."

Ruby stayed quiet a moment. "Yes, I see the spot you mean. Billie, are you on board with that?"

"I am," she said without hesitation while she took out the fake diamonds from her pocket and put them in the glove compartment. "You have protective gear in the SUV?" she asked him.

"Plenty," he assured her. Of course, no amount of gear could prevent them from being killed, but they could make it harder for a sniper to land a fatal shot.

"Your ETA?" Ruby asked.

He checked the GPS. "About thirty minutes."

Which meant after they parked, it would give Billie and him about twenty minutes to thread their way through that ditch and then the trees to get to Victoria so they could meet the kidnappers' deadline.

But it was possible that Victoria might not even be there.

Presley had to shove that aside, too. This was a step in getting her back safely. And that meant trying to keep at least one of the kidnappers alive, so he or she could be questioned. If these were hired thugs, then Presley needed to know the identity of their boss. He always carried some zip ties in his pocket that he could use to restrain one of these SOBs if necessary.

"Drone feed coming in," Ruby said. "I'll send it to your monitor."

That happened in a blink, and Presley saw the drone skimming over the treetops. Of course, in that part of central Texas, there wasn't much of anything else.

The aerial view gave him a good indication of just how thick the woods were, and where there weren't trees, there was dense underbrush. This wasn't a place for a leisurely stroll. It was a remote part of the rugged Hill Country with steep limestone bluffs hidden in the woods. A fall from one of those would be deadly.

They continued to drive, and in the background, Presley could hear Ruby continuing to field calls and texts. She was a general readying her troops for battle. Except there'd be another general on this particular field, and Presley had to wonder if that was meant to add some chaos for the bosses to be on scene. Maybe the killer thought

Owen and Ruby would butt heads and lose focus on the mission.

But that would never happen.

Not for Ruby, anyway. And he couldn't imagine the DV Whisperer falling for it either.

He continued to drive, the minutes seemingly in hyper speed since both time and the landscape were flying by. The drone was continuing to do its thing, too, giving them views of the area. What Presley wasn't seeing though were any signs of the kidnappers or Victoria.

No surprise there.

The kidnappers would have had everything in place before the ransom demand call had even been made. Their vehicle was likely tucked away somewhere out of view from the drone.

"This could be another wild goose chase," Billie muttered, voicing the concern that was racing through his head.

It's what they'd done at his childhood home. Billie and he had rushed there only to find Victoria's finger. Was there another part of her waiting at this location?

Presley had to shove that possibility aside.

Victoria was his mother in only DNA, but it twisted at him to think of her being tortured. And for what? So that some sick SOB could get revenge or eliminate her so there'd be no competition for their daddy's money?

"Someone's there," Presley blurted when he saw the motorcycle pull to a stop off the side of the road about a half mile from the creek.

Billie zoomed in on the drone feed to show a heavily muscled, dark-haired man in camo pants and a black tee. He looked like a bouncer you wouldn't want to cross paths with.

"That's Hayes Brodie," Billie said.

"Yes," Ruby verified. "He'll be approaching the site from the south of the creek. Owen from the east. Angel, from the north. That leaves the west side for Billie and you. I'll be coming in behind you once I arrive. Obviously, friendly fire rules are in effect."

Again, that was no surprise. Not with six operatives in the vicinity. That meant even if he had a kidnapper in his line of sight, Presley would have to wait to make sure he had a clean shot.

The kidnapper had probably planned it that way to stop Maverick Ops and Strike Force from coming in with guns blazing. Not that they would have since the person most likely to be in the middle of this was Victoria.

Presley continued to drive, and he soon passed the motorcycle. No sign of Hayes though, which was probably a good thing. It wasn't a smart idea to be out in the open for long.

When he reached the rock cluster, Presley pulled off the side of the road, and he reached into the back of the SUV to bring out two Kevlar vests, complete with bullet-resistant neck guards. They were a pisser to wear since they were damn uncomfortable, like wearing a thick dog collar, but the guards could save them from a neck shot. The vest would do the same for their chests.

Presley pulled out leg guards next. Again, they were uncomfortable, but Billie and he put them on, along with helmets. The final step was to grab some extra weapons and ammo.

Billie already had a primary and backup weapon, but she took a sheathed Bowie knife and shoved it into the waist of her pants. Presley did the same, and he grabbed a third gun for himself, along with a pair of tiny binoculars that he knew had thermal capabilities. If the kidnappers had Victoria hidden in the trees, he might be able to use the binoculars to spot her.

He grabbed his phone, inserting it into a slot on the sleeve of his shirt. The position would allow him to keep watch of the screen for the drone feed. That could come in handy if for some reason they had to detour off the projected course.

"Earbuds going in now," he told Ruby as Billie and he inserted them. That would keep them in constant voice contact with Ruby.

Presley didn't waste any time saying things like be careful to Billie. Neither did she. Once they were fully armed and geared up, they bolted from the SUV, both of them hurrying to the ditch. Presley had braced himself for gunfire, but it didn't come.

Thankfully, it hadn't rained in a while, and the ditch was not only empty, the mud had dried to a hard rock-like surface. Also, it was deep enough that they didn't have to commando crawl for the quarter of a mile. They were able to crouch down and move fairly fast.

The helmets had a huge disadvantage of blocking out some sounds so Presley had to stay vigilant. He knew that Billie was doing the same behind him. They kept watching, kept moving while Presley also made glances at his phone screen. He didn't see anyone.

"Angel and Owen are at the location," he heard Ruby say through the earbud. "They'll be in place in ten minutes."

Presley figured Billie and he would beat them there. Then they could hunker down and try to spot the kidnappers or Victoria.

Their luck didn't hold out with the ditch, and they lost some of the depth. So much so that they did indeed have to resort to a commando crawl. That added an extra minute or two to their arrival, but they soon reached a thick cluster of trees that overlooked the creek, the bridge, and the road itself. It was such a good spot, and Presley had thought the kidnappers might be there, but then he realized there were many spots just like these all around him.

And the kidnappers could be in one of them.

Billie and he dropped belly down onto the ground, and while she kept watch around them, Presley used the binoculars. Like the rest of the Maverick Ops' gear, these were definitely advanced technology. They fit in the palm of his hand, but he expanded them to view the woods. And he saw plenty of small heat sources.

Wildlife. Probably squirrels or rabbits.

He continued to pan around the woods, but the panning came to a screeching halt when he looked not at the woods but at the creek itself. It was shallow, only about a foot deep, and thick trees with low branches canopied the spot. In the center of that, he saw something.

The woman.

She was on her knees, her hands tied behind her back, and even though he couldn't see her feet, he was betting they were tied too. She had on both a gag and a blindfold, but he still recognized her.

Victoria.

Presley hadn't known what his reaction would be, but it was a fierce one. It felt as if a Mack truck had slammed into him.

"Hostage in sight," he whispered so that Ruby would know.

"I don't have a visual on her," Ruby was quick to say.

"At my eleven o'clock. The trees might be obscuring the drone feed."

Which he figured wasn't by accident. No. This spot had likely been chosen with that in mind.

Presley was about to tell Ruby that Victoria was alive and there were no signs of the kidnappers, but the sound of the voice stopped him.

"Billie and Presley, you came," the cartoon voice boomed. The SOB must have had it on a loudspeaker. "Good. You followed the rules."

Presley waited for the dick to spell out how this exchange would take place. But that didn't happen. Because all hell broke loose.

CHAPTER EIGHT

———— ☆ ————

Billie didn't hear just a single gunshot but rather a barrage of gunfire, and the bullets came right at Presley and her.

Some of the shots flew over their heads and some smacked into the boulders they were using for cover. If Presley and she hadn't already been flat on the ground, they would have been hit.

"Are you both okay?" Ruby asked.

"Yeah, for now," Presley answered.

He had to practically shout for his voice to carry over the sound of the gunfire. And the shots still weren't stopping. The gunmen had to be using some kind of rapid-fire assault rifles.

"Good," Ruby responded. "Stay down and let these assholes keep shooting at you. Fire up in the air every now and then to make them believe you're shooting back."

Presley did just that. He lifted his gun to the sky, his gaze sweeping around, no doubt to make sure the drone wasn't there. And he fired.

"Keep their attention on the two of you," Ruby added. "Once I know the shooters' locations,

I'll try to get Angel, Hayes, and Owen in place to take them out. Can you see the hostage?"

"Yeah," Presley repeated. "Victoria's on her knees in the creek. Tied, gagged, and blindfolded. If we return fire, she'll be caught right in the middle of this gunfight."

Which might have been the kidnappers' intentions all along. Especially if the kidnappers were working for one of Victoria's stepkids or Jesep.

Billie tried to get a visual on the shooters, but it was impossible for her to lean out from the boulder. The equipment she was wearing was bullet-resistant, but that didn't mean the shooters wouldn't get lucky.

There were at least two of them firing nonstop. Had to be because Billie could tell that the bullets were coming from two different angles. One was coming from the west, the direction where her boss would soon be if he wasn't there already. The other shots, from the northwest which meant it was close to the area Angel would be approaching.

"The drone is trying to locate the position of the shooters," Ruby let them know. "But they must be well hidden."

Billie could see that on the screen of Presley's phone. The only thing the drone was picking up was the heavy tree cover.

"Shit," Presley growled.

The alarm raced through Billie when she

glanced over at him and saw that he was peering out from the boulder. And the gunman took advantage of that. A bullet skipped off the top of his helmet, causing them both to curse. If it'd been a direct hit, it could have caused a concussion.

"Victoria's fallen into the water," Presley blurted. "I can't tell if she's been hit or not, but depending on how her feet are tied, she might not be able to get up. She could drown."

Billie cursed, too, and then had her own look —a maneuver that earned her a bullet skim to the helmet as well. Victoria was indeed face down in the creek, and the current wasn't working in her favor.

The water was coming right at her.

Added to that, the kidnappers must have had her anchored in such a way that she couldn't get up. Her body was flailing around, and it was obvious she was in serious distress.

Billie fired a shot up into the air. And she cursed some more when she saw the drone still hadn't found the shooters.

"We have to rescue the hostage," Presley said a split second before Billie had been about to blurt out the same thing.

Ruby hesitated for only a moment. "Go in," she ordered.

Billie had faced gunfire before, but certainly nothing like this, and she had to hope her protective gear would keep her alive. Had to hope, too, that all of Presley's and her training would be enough to get to Victoria and save her. Billie didn't want Presley to have to watch his mother die.

"You go to your left," Presley told her. "I'll go to my right. We move fast and dive behind the nearest cover," he added, sparing her a glance. "Wash, rinse, repeat until the job is done."

That meant he'd need to get across the creek and onto the bank so he could then move closer to Victoria. It'd be too dangerous for him just to charge forward from here to her location. Added to that, trudging through water would be slow which would make him a very easy target. It was best for him to dart across here where the water was shallow and hurry behind cover.

It'd been the exact plan she had in mind, except with her taking on the more dangerous route of crossing the creek. Still, it made sense for Presley to do it because he was already on that side.

While this did feel like a potential suicide mission, they did have some things working in their favor. With Victoria down, there was a lesser chance of her being hit. And the other thing they had on their side was they weren't alone. Soon, Owen, Angel and Hayes would be able to join in the attack.

Dragging in a quick breath, Billie scrambled out from behind the boulder. It didn't surprise her when the gunfire came at her, several bullets whizzing way too close to her before she could drop down behind another rock.

She didn't stay there. Couldn't. She had to get

closer so she could try to protect Presley once he reached Victoria.

Billie darted out again, and as expected, she drew more gunfire. She felt a shot skim over her neck guard, and even though the bullet didn't get through, it still packed a punch. She nearly fell before she could get behind a tree.

She glanced in Presley's direction and saw that he was going full steam ahead. He was already across the creek and onto the bank. And he wasn't stopping.

"Owen has visual on your shooter, Billie," she heard Ruby say. "Stay put for just a second while he takes him out."

Good. Billie was all for one less shooter, but she wished her boss had been able to eliminate the one firing at Presley. He was the one in the most danger now. Victoria, too, since she was still in the water. Billie could see that the woman was managing to lift her head up to get in some air, but the creek water just kept rushing at her, covering her face again and again.

She heard the sound of a different kind of gunfire. Not a barrage but two shots. Owen. He must have succeeded in killing the shooter because the shots stopped coming her way.

And that meant now she could help Presley.

She could do that by drawing his shooter's attention to her until Angel could get to him.

Billie darted out from cover, but she didn't sprint to the nearest tree. She let the shooter see her, and thankfully, it worked. The shots came. Man, did they. One skipped off the shoulder of her vest, but another smacked into her side.

The pain roared through her. The burning, the crushing pressure from the shot. Fighting for breath, Billie had to drop down, and she had one thought on her mind. That she hoped what she'd done had been enough to give Presley a fighting chance.

Staying on her back, she hurried to try to get the vest off her since the now lodged bullet was burning a hole in her. Normally, removing a vest would be an easy task, but there was nothing easy about this with the pain consuming her and with the air still not getting into her lungs.

Somehow, she managed to peel off the vest, and she immediately turned enough so she could try to see Presley. She couldn't. And she suspected he was behind one of the trees. The shooter was firing nonstop again.

Victoria was no longer flailing around. She was motionless, her face down in the water. That got Billie moving again. Not easily, but she readied herself to move out from cover so she'd be a target again.

Without the vest, she would almost certainly be killed.

But Billie was going for it anyway.

"Angel's in place to take out the second shooter," Ruby said through the earbud.

If Billie had had the breath to make a sound,

she would have cheered instead, she dropped back onto the ground and waited. She didn't have to wait long. She heard the two shots. Kill shots.

And the gunfire stopped.

Ruby's voice cut through the silence that followed. "An ambulance is on the way. Is the hostage alive?"

Billie rolled over so she could see. And what she saw was Presley tearing out from behind a tree and rushing into the creek. He seemed to move at a speed much faster than humanly possible, and the moment he reached Victoria, he yanked her out of the water and into his arms.

"She's not breathing," Presley called out.

Billie forced herself to move, and she managed to get to her feet. She staggered her way toward Presley as she watched him put a limp, lifeless Victoria on the bank of the creek. He didn't waste a second starting cutting the duct tape from her hands so he could get her on her back and start CPR.

Angel seemed to come out of nowhere. Owen, too, and they both raced toward Presley and Victoria. Billie did the same, though she wasn't moving anywhere as fast as they were. She kept watch around them, just in case there was a third shooter who was waiting to gun them all down now that they were out in the open.

But no shots came.

Just the frantic sounds that came with the CPR. Owen did the chest compression while Presley breathed air into Victoria's mouth.

The seconds crawled by. An eternity. And the sickening dread went through Billie as she was starting to believe they had failed. That this had all been for nothing. That another woman had died on Presley's and her watch.

Billie said a whole lot of prayers as she staggered her way through the creek. She had just made it to the others when she heard a sound. Not gunfire this time. But a welcome sound.

Victoria gasped for air and started to cough.

Alive.

———— ☆ ————

CHAPTER NINE

———— ☆ ————

Presley sat in the corner of the waiting room in the Outlaw Ridge Hospital and watched the flurry of activity that went along with a situation like this. Organized chaos.

Familiar ground from his days as a cop.

The local sheriff, Marty Bonetti, and his deputies were scattered around the waiting room, taking statements from Owen, Angel, Hayes, Billie, and even Ruby, who'd arrived shortly after the ambulance had brought Victoria here. Presley had already given his statement and had been happy to follow the sheriff's order to take a seat and wait. With the spent adrenaline claiming a good portion of his energy, he didn't mind just chilling for a while.

Too bad he couldn't get his mind to chill right along with his exhausted body. But nope. The thoughts and images were coming nonstop. Of the gunfire. Of Victoria damn near dying before he could get to her. Of Billie as he'd seen her collapse after being shot in the vest.

Thankfully, Billie was okay even though she

was going to have a hell of a bruise on her side for a while. Still, it was better a bruise than a bullet wound, and there'd been plenty of opportunities for the shooters to hit various parts of them that hadn't been protected. A shot to the hands or feet would have prevented them from fighting back and rescuing the hostage.

Victoria was physically going to be okay as well. Probably. The EMTs hadn't offered that somewhat iffy prognosis while they'd been loading her into the ambulance, but Victoria had been semi-conscious—and in shock. She had cuts, bruises, and was missing the tip of her right pinkie finger. She was still being examined to find out if she had internal injuries.

According to the brief report he'd gotten from the EMTs after they'd handed Victoria off to the hospital medical staff, Victoria hadn't said a whole lot in the ambulance, but she had made a couple of things clear. She was grateful for being rescued and she hadn't seen her kidnappers' faces. They'd kept her blindfolded the entire time they'd had her.

Ruby finished up with Sheriff Bonetti and started making her way across the room toward him. Owen and she exchanged a long glance. Not exactly a friendly one, which made Presley wonder again what had gone on between them. Maybe it was nothing more than business differences, what with Ruby walking the thin blue line and Owen often crossing it.

At least those were the rumors, anyway.

But Presley thought of what Billie had said, about Owen's daughter being murdered by a domestic abuser. That sort of trauma could cause a severe thirst for justice. Presley knew because he had it for his adopted mom. However, with her killer dead by his own hand, justice just wasn't in the cards.

Was that why he'd been so desperate to save Victoria?

Maybe.

She wasn't his mother, not in the ways that mattered, but Presley hadn't wanted to fail at bringing her home and getting justice for her. He'd succeeded at the first part, but the second, well, he had a lot of work to do to make that happen.

Ruby sank down in the seat next to him. "Good job," she said. "Once the sheriff clears you to leave, you need to take some time off. At least the rest of the day," she added after she must have seen the argument in his eyes. "It's just common sense. You're almost certainly bone tired, and you need to eat and get some rest. You can start back on the investigation first thing in the morning."

Rather than directly disobey an order, Presley decided it was a good time not to respond with other than a grunt. The sound could have meant anything. Or nothing.

Ruby gave him that flat-eyed boss look. "Any injuries you didn't tell the EMTs about?"

Presley shook his head.

He wouldn't mention that his shoulder was

throbbing. Or that he had the headache from hell from the bullets hitting his safety helmet. He'd had far worse in less dangerous situations.

"You got a text when you were talking to the sheriff," he pointed out. "An update on the kidnappers?"

Her sigh told him that she'd guessed about his unspoken injuries. "It was. The county CSIs IDed them right away with fingerprint matches. Ellis and Craig Dumfries. Brothers, age twenty-nine and thirty-one from Bulverde." A town not far from San Antonio or Outlaw Ridge. "Long rap sheets, starting back when they were juveniles. And before you ask, there are no obvious ties to any of our suspects."

Hell. He'd been hoping the connection would be loud and clear so the cops could make an arrest.

"There's no sign of the kidnappers' vehicle," Ruby went on, "but the CSIs are expanding their search."

Good. But if they didn't find a vehicle, it could mean someone, maybe the kidnappers' boss, had already driven it away.

"Those two had some serious firepower," Presley muttered. "And the set-up was solid except for one thing. They didn't seem to anticipate that we'd have backup with us."

"Yes. They might not have been aware of it because Owen's man, Hayes, disabled some cameras along the road in both directions. He did that with drone strikes before he even arrived. So, it's possible the kidnappers didn't see Owen, Angel, and him coming."

Well, good for Hayes. Presley made a mental note to thank the man though he didn't exactly look the friendly, willing to accept thanks sort.

"There were two more cameras by the creek," Ruby went on. "But one was directed at Victoria and the other was panning the general area where Billie and you first arrived."

At the mention of Victoria's name, Presley got another flurry of those blasted thoughts. He knew this was all part of the post-mission process. It wasn't easy to put to bed all the little pieces of the ordeal.

Especially the part about him carrying Victoria's limp body to the bank.

"A friend of a friend is a nurse here," Ruby went on, "and I got an unofficial update on Victoria's medical condition. She's stable and gave a brief statement to the sheriff before she was taken away for some x-rays."

Presley figured Ruby would be able to find out whatever Victoria ended up telling the sheriff. Just because the woman hadn't seen her kidnappers, it didn't mean she didn't know something about them that could lead to who'd hired them.

Because they had been hired.

Presley could feel that in his gut. These two losers hadn't acted alone in this.

"I saw the guns they used for the attack," Presley said. "They used AR-15s with lightning link modifications. About two grand each with the modifications. Anything in their bank accounts to verify they could have bought something that expensive?"

"Nothing," Ruby verified. "Of course, they could have had cash squirreled away that they used." She didn't sound as if she believed that any more than he did.

"What did Jesep, Olivia, and Ari say when you let them know Victoria had been rescued?" Presley asked.

"I spoke to Jesep, and he thanked me. He's on his way here."

That gave him a jolt of fresh alarm. "If he hired the kidnappers, he might try to finish her off in the hospital."

"He won't get the chance. I'm having Angel guard her for a while." Her gaze went to his. "You're too close to this. Best if you step back and…deal. It had to have shaken you when you found out she was your bio-mom."

"It did, but I can still do the job," he argued.

But he wasn't sure he actually wanted bodyguard duty. Not until Victoria at least knew who he was. Because then, she might have to do her own dealing, and he'd rather not be around for that.

Something must have caused her to drop him off at the fire station, and it sure as hell wasn't lack of funds. She came from money, lots and lots of it. Of course, her rich folks likely wouldn't have approved of her having a kid. And then there'd been the bio-father angle. It was possible the guy had been the one who'd ditched Presley.

That left another possibility.

The worst of the bunch. Because maybe Victoria had had all the money and support in the world, but she simply hadn't wanted him. Hadn't cared enough about him to even put him up for adoption. Even as an adult, that stung.

"How about you handling what you learned about Victoria?" Ruby asked, "And feel free to tell me to mind my own business."

"It's your business because I work for you. You have to know you can trust me in any situation where you assign me." He paused. "But I'll have to get back to you on how I'm handling it."

Ruby nodded as if that'd been the exact answer she'd expected. Presley didn't get a chance to say more because he saw Billie step away from the deputy and head their way. He watched her movements, looking for any signs of pain. And it was there all right. She winced a little when she sat down on the other side of him.

"Good job on the mission," Ruby told her, and she stood. "I'll try to get some updates from the sheriff."

Ruby went in that direction, and what she'd said likely wasn't BS. She probably did want to get some intel, but Presley suspected her quick departure was to give Billie and him a moment alone.

Presley studied Billie's face, cursing the new bruise that she now had in addition to the black eye. And it wasn't the only bruise. He knew there was another one where the bullet had hit her vest. He hadn't gotten a look at that one, but figured it was just below her right breast.

Mercy, he wanted to pull her into his arms. Gently though. He wanted to have just that body to body contact with her. But this definitely wasn't the time or the place, not with both of their bosses and half of the local police force in the room.

"Please tell me you got some pain meds," he murmured, moving a strand of her hair off her cheek.

"I got it. Not sure I'll take it. How about you? How bad is your headache?" she asked.

Despite everything, including the damn headache, he smiled. "It's a good day. We won. Sort of," he tacked onto that. "We didn't get the big asshole who hired the little assholes who tried to kill us."

She sighed, nodded. "I heard that Jesep, Olivia, and Ari are on the way here to the hospital."

"Yeah. Angel's guarding Victoria."

That put some relief on Billie's face, and she continued to study him. "I have to take at least a mandatory twelve hours off since I was involved in a shooting. Owen's rules," she added.

"Ruby has a similar one," he let her know. "Why don't we do our downtime together? My house is only about twenty minutes from here."

There. He'd thrown out an invitation that he figured she'd turned down. She didn't.

"Okay," she said after pausing only a heartbeat. "And just know that I could really use a hug from you right now."

Presley smiled, and he did a big assed no-no by leaning in and brushing his mouth over hers. Billie certainly didn't push him away. In fact, she appeared to be on the verge of kissing him right back, but the sound of approaching footsteps put a halt to that.

He looked up and saw Owen Striker looming over them.

Emphasis on *looming*. The guy definitely looked Delta Force, and not ex or retired either. He seemed more than capable of being on active duty.

And kicking some serious ass.

Billie started to stand, almost as if she were about to come to attention, but Owen motioned her back down. "I just wanted to check on you before I head out." He volleyed glances at both of them.

Presley braced himself for Owen to mention that kiss. No way in hell had he missed it. But he didn't.

"Downtime," Owen spelled out. "Get it while you can. This investigation will heat up again when we find out who's behind the kidnapping."

Owen had barely finished that when there were more footsteps, and this time both Presley and Billie got to their feet when they saw it was a doctor heading straight for them.

Hell. Presley hoped Victoria hadn't taken a turn for the worst because the doc didn't look as if he was the bearer of good news.

"Presley Nolan and Billie Cooper?" the doctor asked. According to his nametag, he was Isaac Jenkins.

Billie and he nodded.

"Mrs. Wessington would like to see both of you," the doctor said, and Presley felt some of the tension ease up in his chest. "Personally, I think she should hold off on seeing non-family members because she should be resting. But she insisted."

Dr. Jenkins turned, instructing them to follow him. They did, threading their way down a hall that fed off the waiting area. Presley refused to even guess why the woman wanted to see him. He just kept walking, and he felt Billie take hold of his hand and give it a gentle squeeze. Presley squeezed right back.

There was a sign for ICU, but thankfully the doctor didn't lead them in that direction. Instead, he took them to a room directly across from a small nurses' station. Angel wasn't here yet, but he no doubt would be once he'd finished his statement.

The doctor opened the door, and Presley immediately caught a glimpse of Victoria. Her face was a riot of bruises and scrapes, and those injuries were the only color in her skin. The rest of her was ashy pale.

Along with the bandage on her hand, there were more on her forehead and both arms. Stitches, too. Some along her hairline and on her chin. The corners of her mouth were cracked and raw, probably from the gag the kidnappers had forced her to wear.

No wonder the doctor hadn't wanted her to have visitors.

"Presley, Billie," Victoria greeted. Her voice was a rasp, barely audible, but she sat up and motioned for them to come in.

"Please lie back down," the doctor insisted, and he hurried to help her do just that. He also covered her with the thin white blanket that she had shoved to the side. "We were able to reattach Mrs. Wessington's finger, but she needs rest. Five minutes," he warned Billie and Presley. "I'll be right outside the door."

Presley figured the doctor was actually timing this so he went closer, waiting for Victoria to dole out a thank you. Or question them about whether or not she was safe now.

She didn't do either of those.

Victoria looked him straight in the eyes. Eyes that he realized were a genetic copy of his own. "I know who you are, Presley," she muttered, choking back a sob. "You're my son."

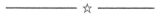

CHAPTER TEN

---- ☆ ----

Billie reached for Presley's hand again. No way could touching him help ease the eruption of emotions he had to be feeling right now. But there was little else she could do.

"Do you want me to leave so you can have a private talk with Victoria?" Billie asked. She couldn't use the term, mother, not with that shock she saw in Presley's eyes.

"No," Presley was quick to say, and Victoria echoed the same.

"I wanted to thank both of you for rescuing me," the woman said. She swallowed hard. "I don't believe the kidnappers ever intended to release me. I think they were going to kill me."

Billie believed the same thing, and she had so many questions for Victoria. Such as why had those two thugs wanted her dead? Why had she been kidnapped in the first place? And had she merely been the bait to get to Presley and her?

But all those questions and more would have to wait.

Because those five minutes were ticking away,

and Presley no doubt needed to ask his birth mom some things as well.

"I, uh, don't expect you to forgive me," Victoria said, her gaze pinned on Presley now. "And I don't expect you to understand why I did what I did."

"Enlighten me," Presley invited.

There was no venom in his voice. In fact, there wasn't much of anything. He'd obviously managed to rein it all in so he could have this conversation.

Which would no doubt be the first of many.

No way were they going to work out thirty-six years in four and a half minutes.

Victoria nodded. "I'm going to assume you ran a thorough background check on me so you already know my parents were wealthy. Old money with equally old-fashioned expectations for their only daughter. I rebelled in oh so many ways." She closed her eyes a moment. "And I got pregnant when I was barely sixteen."

"There's nothing about that in your background check," Presley pointed out.

"No, there wouldn't be because I used a fake ID that my parents provided for my doctor's appointments." She paused. "I also used that fake ID when I gave birth."

Billie felt Presley's hand tighten in hers. "And after giving birth, you left me in a fire station just outside of San Antonio."

Victoria's eyes widened a moment, and it seemed as if she were about to dispute that, but then the objection faded from her expression. "I abandoned you," she finally said.

She didn't add more, and the heavy, uncomfortable silence settled between them for a couple of moments. Presley was the one to break it.

"Who's my bio-father?" he demanded, and this time, there was some anger in tone and body language.

Billie totally got that. Had their situations been reversed, she would have felt the same. And she would have wanted to know what Presley had just asked.

"Your father," Victoria muttered.

Certainly, the woman must have anticipated the question, but she was taking her time answering. She'd just opened her mouth when there was a shout outside the door.

"I will see my wife now," the man yelled. *Jesep.* "And you can't keep me from her."

"Step aside," another man snarled.

Ari.

The two were likely speaking to the doctor or maybe even Angel.

Panic raced over Victoria's face, and she frantically shook her head. "Please don't tell them what we were just talking about," she managed to blurt before the door flew open.

Dr. Jenkins gave Victoria an apologetic glance before he stepped to the side to reveal not only Jesep and Ari but also Olivia. "I'll call security and have them removed if you're not up to seeing them."

"I'm up to it," Victoria insisted, and she plastered on what Billie was pretty sure was a fake smile. "Come in," she added, aiming a glance at Billie and Presley.

That glance seemed to be both a plea for them to keep her secret and a promise that the conversation wasn't over.

Jesep led his kids into the room, and they all ignored Presley and her as they went to Victoria's bedside. Jesep didn't kiss his wife. In fact, he didn't touch her. None of the three did. They just gathered around her bed, staring down at her.

"Mrs. Wessington experienced severe trauma," Dr. Jenkins insisted. "You can only stay a couple of minutes. And you two have to leave," he added to Presley and her.

Presley gave Victoria one last look, and Billie and he stepped out into the hall with the doctor. What he didn't do was shut the door.

"It's possible Mrs. Wessington is still in danger," Presley whispered to the doctor, and he fired off a text while he continued to keep an eye on Victoria and the others. "I have a colleague, Angel DeLuca, who'll be protecting her, and he'll be here any minute."

The doctor's shoulders went stiff. "Is she in danger from her family?" He, too, kept his voice at a whisper.

"Possibly. She's not to be left alone with any of them, understand?" Presley stated.

Dr. Jenkins' nod was a little shaky, but there

was still plenty of resolve in it. Good. Angel would no doubt be thorough in his bodyguard duties, but it didn't hurt to have someone else watching out for the woman.

As Presley had said, Angel soon appeared in the hall, and he made a beeline toward them. Presley did the introductions, and they all turned to look at Victoria. She, too, was having a whispered conversation, and judging from Ari's, Olivia's, and Jesep's expressions, they didn't care much for what she was saying.

"I'll take care of her," Angel said like a promise, and he stepped into the room.

Jesep immediately whirled toward Angel, doling out a scowl to him. "Who the hell are you?"

"Your wife's bodyguard," Angel calmly replied.

Jesep's scowl deepened while Ari and Olivia looked on. "Well, you can just leave. I'll get my own security for my wife."

"I'm not going anywhere," Angel fired back, and he was doling out his own scowl. His was a lot meaner looking that Jesep's. "Your wife is under police protection, and I'm a contracted security specialist. You don't have a say in it. Neither do the two of you," he added, giving Ari and Olivia a glance.

"We'll just see about that," Jesep snarled, taking out his phone.

Victoria caught onto his hand to stop him from making a call. "I asked for the protection," she said. That was possibly a lie though Billie supposed she could have done it in the ambulance or after she'd arrived at the hospital.

"Why the hell would you do that?" Jesep yanked back his hand. "I was told the kidnappers are dead. Aren't they dead?" he asked, aiming that at Billie.

It was a rhetorical question, but Billie answered it anyway. "They are. Ellis and Craig Dumfries."

Victoria made a sound that sounded like a mix of a soft moan or gasp, and it was loud enough to get their attention. Everyone turned toward her.

"What?" Presley said. "Do you know them?"

She shook her head, but there seemed to be some kind of recognition in her eyes. "No. Did you find out why they kidnapped me?"

Presley didn't get a chance to answer that before Jesep spoke first. "Because they're greedy sonsofbitches who thought they could get rich, that's why. And they're dead. That's means you can leave here since you're not in danger."

Victoria nodded and took her time answering. "But I don't feel safe yet. I wanted a bodyguard in case someone else tries to take me."

"You'll be safer at home," Jesep insisted, and his voice was very close to a shout. "Away from this... place. Away from them." He tipped his head to Billie and Presley. "Ari and I can help you get to the car. Come with us."

Dr. Jenkins hurried back into the room, and he stepped between Jesep and Victoria. "Your wife was severely injured. She can't leave."

Jesep seemed ready to gear up to dispute that, but Olivia took him by the arm and eased him back. "Why don't you arrange to have Victoria transported to a hospital in San Antonio? That way, she'll be close to home, and she'll get the medical care she needs."

Jesep glanced around as if figuring out if this was a battle he could win. He must have decided the answer to that was a no because he backed down, and he released a slow breath.

"I'm sorry," Jesep muttered to no one in particular. "I'm just very worried about my wife. She just survived what had to have been a horrible ordeal. We went through a trauma, too, not knowing if she was alive. Not knowing if she'd be allowed to come home."

Billie hoped that wasn't lip service, a spiel meant to get the doctor to let down his guard. No way would Angel fall for it though, and with Victoria confirming that she wanted a bodyguard, then at least she would have some protection even if she was transferred to another hospital.

"Billie, Presley," Victoria said, shifting her attention to them. "Thank you again for rescuing me. I'll be in touch."

It was clearly a goodbye, but they didn't budge.

"I'll be all right," Victoria tacked onto that, glancing at Angel.

Presley stared at her for several long moments before he finally turned and walked away. Billie was right there with him, and she seriously doubted he was ready to face his boss and the cops, who were no doubt still in the ER waiting area. She spotted the sign for a breakroom just ahead, and she took hold of his hand to pull him inside. Thankfully, it was empty, but so they'd have a little privacy, she moved him to the corner away from the door.

"Feel free to vent," Billie offered.

She thought he was going to take her up on that. That riot of emotions was still there in his eyes, vibrating in every part of him. But he didn't vent. He sighed, closed his eyes and leaned against the wall.

"Shit," he finally said.

"That expresses my sentiment, too."

She didn't pepper him with questions about how he was doing or what he was feeling. Billie just waited him out, and little by little, she felt some of the tension melt away.

"After my mom was killed," he finally said, "I, of course, gave some thought to my bio-mom. But I never wanted to find her. I always figured if she abandoned me that she wanted nothing to do with me."

She heard the hurt that was still there over that abandonment. It likely always would be. Billie had felt some of that when her own dad had stepped out of her life after her parents had divorced. It was one of those little holes in the heart that never healed.

"I don't know what to do about Victoria," Presley said. "I don't know what to feel."

"You don't have to work it all out now," Billie assured him. "It can be a process with no timetable on it."

One that would likely involve learning who his bio-dad was, too. Victoria had seemed to be on the verge of spilling that when Jesep and her stepkids had burst into the room.

"Thanks," he muttered, opening his eyes and meeting her gaze. "I'm sorry you got dragged into all this personal crap."

"No need to apologize." Yes, it'd been a shock when she had first been pulled into this, but as Billie looked at him now, she was glad she had been here with him for this ordeal. They weren't besties by any means, but there was a connection between them that made her care about him.

And want him.

But for now, she was focusing on the caring part when she pulled him into her arms for a hug. He immediately slid his arms around her and pulled her to him.

And he kissed her.

It was long and slow. A no pressure kind of kiss. Or at least it would have been had it come from anyone else. But with Presley, the heat was always going to create an urgency even when the kiss shouldn't even be happening.

They were hardly in a private place. Someone could come walking in at any moment. Added to that, Presley likely wasn't in the right frame of mind for this since less than two hours earlier, he'd had to rescue his own mother.

Still, they didn't stop, and the kiss raged on.

Presley snapped her closer to him, until they were body to body. Pressed against each other. Until everything else except this faded into the background. Until Billie had to force herself to step back and regain, well, everything. Her breath, her composure. Her sanity. Because Presley and that scalding kiss had certainly muddled her brain.

They stood there, breaths gusting, hearts racing, and stared at each other. She wasn't sure how much time had passed, but she yanked herself out of the kiss trance when she heard the footsteps. A moment later, Olivia appeared in the doorway.

"Oh, sorry for interrupting," Olivia muttered. Even though Presley and she were no longer touching, Olivia had clearly picked up on the vibe in the room.

Billie picked up on a vibe, too, from Olivia, and it was one of concern.

"Is Victoria all right?" Billie asked.

"Uh, yes. Well, I guess as okay as can be expected. I can't imagine the hell those two men put her through."

The words were right, but Billie had the same thought she had with Jesep—she hoped it was the real deal and not some façade.

"They cut off a piece of her finger," Olivia

muttered, and she went to the vending machine. She used her credit card to buy a bottle of water. Once she had it open, she took a long drink. "My father's not as much of an asshole as he appears to be," she went on. "He uses anger to mask his fear."

Neither Presley nor Billie responded to that. Since it seemed as if the woman was in a talking mood, Billie just decided to hear her out and listen to what she had to say. Maybe she would spill something that would help them ID the person who'd hired those kidnappers.

Heck, it could even be Olivia.

"I need to know something," Olivia went on, still guzzling that water as if she'd just crossed a desert. "Why did those men ask for the two of you to deliver the ransom? How are you connected to my stepmother?"

Oh, that was a question Billie figured Presley wouldn't answer. And he didn't. Well, he didn't give a truthful answer anyway.

"We don't know why they pulled us into this," he said. "But it's something we're investigating."

Olivia stayed quiet a moment. "So, it's possible that choosing you had nothing to do with Victoria, that the kidnappers could have been after you instead?"

Presley shrugged. "We don't know," he repeated. "Trust me though, learning that is the top priority. The cops, Maverick Ops, and Strike Force are all investigating. If someone hired those men to take Victoria, we'll find him or her and bring them to justice."

It sounded like a warning. Or a threat. And Olivia seemed to grasp that they were looking at her. At her entire family.

"I see," Olivia muttered. "Well, good." She recapped the bottle and tossed it in the trash before she added a barely audible goodbye and walked out.

Presley didn't move. He stood still until they could no longer hear Olivia's footsteps, and then he went to the trash to retrieve the bottle.

Billie raised an eyebrow. "You have plans for that?"

"I do. Jesep, Ari, and Olivia still haven't given the cops DNA samples. This is a start. The CSIs are already processing the clothes and belongings of our dead guys, and I'll give them this. If there's any Wessington DNA on them, then that'll give us some ammo so the cops can make an arrest."

———— ☆ ————

CHAPTER ELEVEN

--- ☆ ---

Working his way through his third cup of coffee, Presley sat at his desk in his home office, fighting hard to tamp down the firestorm of thoughts and emotions that kept burning away at him.

Something he'd done throughout the night.

And it was the reason he hadn't gotten much sleep. Billie probably hadn't either in the guestroom just up the hall. Still, they'd been exhausted when they'd arrived at his house and had gone off to their respective rooms.

Alone.

Because, hey, exhaustion and so very much to process.

Presley was still doing the processing thing, but he didn't want to deal with how he felt about Victoria being his bio-mother. Or about the shit the kidnappers had put her through. He didn't want to deal with the mental exhaustion from hell that he was having right now. Or keep thinking about that scalding kiss that Billie and he had shared at the hospital.

He just needed to focus on the investigation.

On finding who'd hired those kidnappers. That was it. Nothing more.

But it was impossible to shut out everything else, and at that moment, he felt like a hamster on a never-ending wheel. He suspected Billie was having a similar experience as she worked on a laptop on the sofa.

Since they'd gotten up shortly after sunrise and jumped straight into work, hardly more than ten minutes had gone by without an alert from incoming texts and emails. Some were from Angel to let them know that Jesep was still pushing to get Victoria released. And was thankfully failing at that. Mainly because Angel and Ruby were pushing right back to keep her where she was. Simply put, they weren't sure Victoria was going to be safe in the *loving* arms of her family.

Another ding to indicate a new email. This one was an update from the CSIs who were processing the creek. So far, they'd found squat that would help. Still, Presley was glad they were in the loop because that squat could turn into something big in a blink if the kidnappers had managed to leave any clues behind to prove someone had hired them or if they'd worked alone.

He'd barely finished reading that one when another came in from the Outlaw Ridge sheriff, Marty Bonetti. He was friends with Owen, so Owen had convinced him to copy Billie and him on any and all of the developments in the investigation. That's why they were also getting preliminary reports from the ME who was dealing with the dead brothers, Craig and Ellis Dumfries.

This latest report, however, was to give a summary of the death notification to Craig and Ellis' next of kin.

Again, squat.

Their mother was dead, and their dad had apparently left when the boys had been young. The mother had remarried, and their stepfather, Joe Malloy, had said he hadn't seen neither Craig nor Ellis in nearly two years, that the brothers had cut off communications with him when he'd refused to bail them out of jail for what would have been a third time.

According to one of the deputies, the stepfather had been visibly upset when questioned about the kidnapping, but he hadn't been able to offer them any info on anyone that his stepsons might have been working with. However, Joe had given them the name of Craig and Ellis' older brother, Damon, and Sheriff Bonetti was trying to track him down.

Of course, reading all of that had put Presley right back on the hamster wheel, where he couldn't shut out his thoughts about how Victoria had reacted when she'd abandoned him.

"Abandoned," he muttered. He swiveled his chair around to face Billie. "Victoria seemed surprised, or something, when I mentioned being left at the fire station as a newborn. Or was that my imagination?" He wasn't sure of pretty much anything when it came to Victoria.

Billie shook her head. "Not your imagination," she confirmed. She set her laptop aside and went closer to him. "And I've been looking into that."

That got his attention. "How?"

"With Strike Force's data mining program." She sighed. "Yes, I know some of the data in it was obtained through hacking, and that Ruby wouldn't approve."

"No, she wouldn't," Presley agreed, and then he immediately asked, "Did you find something?"

"Maybe. I believe when Victoria had you, she used the name Melissa Williams. The date fits anyway with your birth. Melissa Williams didn't exist six months prior to your birth and disappeared shortly thereafter."

That meshed with what Victoria had told them.

"There are no medical records, so maybe her parents had them destroyed. Or she could have done that herself. Maybe she didn't want Jesep to know she'd had a child as a teenager."

"Yeah," he muttered. "But that surprised look in Victoria's eyes make me believe…" He had to stop because there were just too many possibilities. Too many questions.

Billie eased her hip on the desk, took out her phone and pulled up a photo. "Those are Victoria's late parents, Markham and Laura Beaumont."

"Late," he repeated.

"Yes, they both died when Victoria was still in college. Private jet crash," she explained.

Presley studied the stone-faced man and the blonde-haired woman beside him in what was a posed shot at some kind of fancy party. He wanted to curse when he recognized some of his own features in them. His black hair. Hell, even Markham's eyes.

"They look like rich snobs," he concluded.

"They were. And after reading about them, I totally believe there's no way they would have approved of their teenage daughter getting pregnant."

"Yeah, especially getting pregnant by someone not in their social circle." He looked at Billie. "I don't suppose you found any photos of Victoria with a boyfriend or a date."

She shook her head. "But part of the data mining program is connected to the genealogy sites. I could dig around in those. If you find your bio-dad, he might be willing to give you answers that Victoria won't."

He considered it and then said, "No. This feels like a let sleeping dogs lie situation." Presley paused. "Besides, it doesn't matter why I was left at the fire station."

"Maybe." Billie paused, too. "But the kidnappers requested us for a reason, and your bio-parents might have played into that."

Hell. He hadn't even considered that angle.

That was even more reason to try to clear his head and get off this blasted hamster wheel. He'd been trained to look at things objectively, and that's what he had to start doing.

"We'll need to talk to Victoria again," Presley said. "An actual interview. And we need all the pieces to this puzzle."

Billie nodded again. "I'll put in a search through the genealogy sites and let it run since it could take a while. I can also call someone at SAPD and get them to lean on Jesep and Ari for DNA samples. Olivia's sample from the water bottle is at the lab, and we should be getting something back on that soon."

Good. That might not give them any useful info, but Presley wouldn't know that for sure until they had the results. Not just from Olivia but from the clothes Victoria had been wearing while she was kidnapped. In one of the reports that Presley had read, the lab had said the findings on that would be back no later than tomorrow morning.

He reached out, his gaze connecting with Billie's. Both of them sighed at the same time, and that caused Presley to smile. Why, he didn't know. There wasn't a hell of a lot to smile about.

"Thanks," he said.

Her eyebrow rose. "For what?"

"For thinking straight when I can't," he settled for saying. "And for not telling me that kiss at the hospital was a big-assed mistake."

"It could have been a mistake," she countered

but then shrugged. "But it wasn't. If we didn't have this investigation hanging over us, then we might be able to do more of it and see where it takes us."

No way could he blow that off. Presley stood, and in the same motion, he slipped his arm around her waist and pulled her to him.

And he kissed her.

He instantly felt the rush of heat. The rush of pleasure, too, and there were much better things to feel than the worry about the case. Billie must have thought so, too, because she sure as heck didn't put a stop to it. Just the opposite. She wrapped her arms around him, dragging him even closer.

In a blink, they deepened the kiss, and even though Presley had tried to steel himself up for the punch he got from tasting her, he failed big time. The punch came. A welcoming flood of sensations that went right along with the heat.

Of course, her taste and kiss created the urgency that came with the lust. His body instantly wanted more, and he took that more by sliding his hand over the front of her shirt to her breasts. He kept his touch gentle there, aware of the bruise she had to be sporting.

He could have kept touching, kept kissing, too, if there hadn't been another blasted ding. This one from his phone, and it was a text.

Billie slipped out of his grip, easing her arms and her body away from his, and Presley was muttering a bunch of profanity when he checked his phone.

"It's Ruby," he relayed to her, and while the heat was still pressing for the *more* with Billie, he knew it was going to have to wait.

"Hattie went to school with one of the dead kidnappers. Craig Dumfries," Presley summarized. "They even dated for a while, and according to social media, they've stayed in touch over the years despite Craig's criminal history."

Billie nodded. "That might be the connection we're looking for, and it would explain a lot of things."

Yeah, it would. Hattie could have known that Victoria was his bio-mom, and along with Craig and Ellis, she could have orchestrated the kidnapping. Possibly to make Presley suffer if he had been unable to save the woman who'd given birth to him. Maybe to set up a scenario where Billie and he would be killed by the Dumfries brothers. That way, she wouldn't come under suspicion for the murders.

But if that was true, Hattie had left a very sloppy thread with her association with Craig.

"Sheriff Bonetti has already had a phone interview with Hattie," Presley continued to summarize. "Or rather he tried, but Hattie lawyered up in the middle of it so he had to schedule her to come into the Outlaw Ridge police station. Bonetti thinks we should call the woman as well, that she might say something to us in anger that she wouldn't say to him."

"Agreed," Billie was quick to say.

Presley was on the same page, but before he made that call, he fired off a text to Ruby. "Does Hattie know we're aware of her connection to Craig?"

As expected, Ruby replied right away. "She knows. That's the reason she lawyered up. You might not get anywhere talking to her, but I thought you'd want to try anyway."

He did indeed, and after he texted his thanks to Ruby for the info, he located the contact number for Hattie and called her. Presley figured there was a good chance the woman wouldn't even answer, so he was surprised when she took the call on the first ring. However, she didn't say anything.

"Hattie," Presley greeted after a couple of moments, and he put the call on speaker. "I have Billie Cooper here with me, and we'd like to ask you a few questions."

The woman cursed, and it seemed to him that she'd been expecting a call. Just not from him. But from whom? And did it have anything to do with Victoria's kidnapping?

"What the hell do you want, Detective Nolan?" she snarled, making his surname and former rank sound like some kind of nasty rash.

Presley jumped straight to the heart of the matter. "Craig Dumfries," was all he said.

Silence, followed by a single curse word. "What about him?"

"I'm betting you know exactly why I'm calling about him," Presley countered.

Hattie huffed. "I don't, and if you're wanting to play cat and mouse, then you're wasting your time and mine."

He thought she might hang up. She didn't. But Hattie huffed again.

"Did you tell that sheriff I had teamed up with Craig and his brother to kidnap that rich bitch?" Hattie snapped. "Are you the reason he's hauling my ass into an interview?"

"No, your association with Craig is the reason you've been called in," Presley was quick to remind her. "That's what happens when you hang around with known criminals."

"Well, I had no part in what that asshole did," Hattie insisted. "When your former friends get into trouble, are you responsible?" But she didn't wait for an answer. "I didn't help Craig in any way, and I don't appreciate being dragged into this shit. Haven't you and Lieutenant Cooper done enough to ruin my life? Do you have to keep going after me like this?"

"Funny, that was a similar to what I was going to ask you," Presley said. "Did you have Victoria Wessington kidnapped so you could try to get your pound of flesh from Billie and me?"

"I have no idea what you're talking about," Hattie insisted.

"You're sure about that because Craig was definitely involved with the kidnapping. If he wasn't working with you, then who would have helped him put something like this together?"

"His brothers," she spat out. "They could have helped him. Ellis and the other one…uh, Damon. Yes, that was his name. They were tight. So, call him and quit pestering me."

And this time, she did hang up.

"Well, that was productive," Presley muttered. It was sarcasm with a side order of frustration.

Billie made a so-so motion with her hand. "She hesitated when she answered the phone. If she's connected to the kidnapping, maybe she's not actually the person in charge. Maybe she was waiting on a call from the boss."

"True," he admitted. "And she mentioned Damon."

Presley searched through the reports and located the latest update on him. Sheriff Bonetti still hadn't been able to find him. According to his landlord, Damon had moved out a week earlier, right before he was due to be evicted. Like his brothers, he, too, had a criminal record.

And something else.

Known ties to a militia group. *Bingo.* That could have been where Craig and Ellis got their weapons.

He was about to fill Billie in on what he'd just read, but an incoming call cut him off. For a moment, he thought maybe it was Hattie phoning him back.

But it was Angel.

Presley couldn't answer it fast enough. "Is Victoria all right?" he immediately asked.

However, it wasn't Angel who answered.

"It's me, Victoria," she said in a whisper. "Angel was kind enough to let me use his phone since I don't have mine."

"Are you all right?" Presley repeated after he fumbled around with what to say to her. Hell, this was awkward.

"I'm healing," she said after a short pause. Victoria cleared her throat. "Presley, I need to see Billie and you. Because, uh, I think I know who was behind my kidnapping."

———— ☆ ————

CHAPTER TWELVE

---- ☆ ----

It didn't surprise Billie that Presley once again went into the bat out of hell mode as he drove to the hospital. Victoria had dropped a bombshell, and it was the bombshell that Presley and she had wanted.

I think I know who was behind my kidnapping.

Finally, they might get some answers about this ordeal that Victoria had been through. Of course, Presley and she had been through part of it, too, and they needed to know if they were the reason this had happened.

Billie remembered the hatred she'd heard in Hattie's voice, and if Hattie had actually orchestrated the kidnapping, then maybe Victoria had learned that. The kidnappers had held her a long time, and all it took was a slip of the tongue to reveal something that they might not have intended to reveal.

Presley turned into the hospital parking lot and found a space that wasn't far from the ER doors. They hurried in, threading their way to her room, where they saw Angel standing guard at the door. He showed no signs of surprise at seeing them, which meant Victoria had probably told him they were coming.

"Is Jesep or her stepkids around?" Presley asked him.

Angel shook his head. "They all left about an hour ago. Not sure when they'll be back, so whatever Victoria's got to say to you, try to make it fast. She doesn't say much of anything important whenever they're around."

"Does she seem scared of them?" Billie asked.

Angel lifted his shoulder. "Maybe. She sure as hell seems a lot better when they're not here. Don't get me wrong. She needs to be in the hospital, but I don't think she's as weak as she makes out to be to Jesep and his kids."

Interesting, and Billie wanted to know why that was. But Presley and she also needed to take Angel's suggestion of doing this fast.

"It's Billie and me," Presley said, giving a single knock on the door.

"Come in," Victoria replied.

The greeting was quick, and when they stepped into the room, Billie saw what Angel had meant about the woman maybe doing better than she was leading her family to believe. She didn't look the picture of health, but she was fully sitting up, and there was some color other than the bruises on her face.

"Thank you for coming," she said, and even her voice was stronger. She set aside a tablet that someone had obviously brought in for her since their last visit. "I'm not sure how much time we have. Jesep is talking to his doctor to convince him to come to Outlaw Ridge and take over my care."

"You can't just tell him no?" Billie pressed.

Victoria shook her head and seemed to offer a silent apology about that, making Billie wonder if Jesep was abusive to his wife. But that serious topic would apparently have to wait because Presley launched right into the reason for this visit.

"Who's responsible for your kidnapping?" he threw out there.

The woman closed her eyes a moment. "I'm not certain, but I suspect Ari could be behind it."

Bingo. Billie suspected the same thing. Then again, that suspicion also applied to Jesep, Olivia, and Hattie.

"I don't have any proof," Victoria went on a moment later. "But Ari hates me, and I feel in my gut that he would like me out of his father's life."

Billie didn't groan. Not out loud, anyway. But she'd been hoping for more than a gut feeling here.

"Has Ari said or done anything to make you believe he'd hire those kidnappers?" Presley asked.

"No," she said but then paused. "He's been acting strange though. For instance, last week he was talking on the phone when I walked into the room, and he just hung up on the caller. And later that day, he wasn't where he was supposed to be.

He told Jesep he had a business meeting in Austin, but when I spoke to his PA about another matter, she said there was no meeting, that Ari had gone home for the day."

Again, nothing major. Still, Billie couldn't dismiss the fact that Victoria said that Ari hated her. That was motive.

"What about Olivia?" Billie pressed. "How does she feel about you?"

Victoria drew in a weary-sounding breath. "Well, I can't imagine she's pleased with her father's new will."

Billie and Presley exchanged a glance, and it was Presley who spelled out the question. "Olivia knows about that?"

"Yes. Both Ari and she do. Jesep told them in a family meeting. He decided he wanted his kids to earn their own fortunes the way he did through hard work and no trust fund." She clamped her teeth over her bottom lip a moment. "The will has put another wedge between Ari, Olivia, and me."

"*Another*?" Presley questioned. "What other wedges are there?"

"The obvious one of me being the stepmother and Jesep encouraged them to keep me at an emotional distance. He's never wanted them to think of me as a mother, that if they did that, it would somehow replace his first wife."

Billie heard the hurt there. Maybe the resignation, too. What she wasn't hearing was any reason for Victoria to stay married to Jesep.

"When was this meeting to tell Ari and Olivia about the new will?" Billie asked.

"Last month," Victoria muttered, and Billie could tell from the woman's tone and expression that she thought maybe the new will had played into what'd happened to her.

"So, both Ari and Olivia have a reason to want you out of the way," Presley concluded.

Victoria sighed. Nodded.

"And Jesep?" Presley went on. "Does he have a motive?"

"No." That response came quickly, but then she sighed. "Not that I know of anyway. Our life together has been far from perfect, but we've been married for twenty-eight years. He's never asked me for a divorce, and as far as I know, he hasn't cheated."

Not exactly resounding confirmations of a marriage that'd lasted so long. Definitely no mention of love.

"You were young when you married Jesep," Billie commented.

Victoria nodded. "Twenty-four. Jesep was forty-one."

"And you met when you became Olivia's bone marrow donor," Presley added, obviously his attempt to get the woman talking. So far, Victoria wasn't painting a full picture of her life as a Wessington.

"No, I'd met Jesep before that," Victoria corrected. "He and my father were friends and had done business together." Another pause. "Look, I don't expect you to understand this, but my father admired and respected Jesep, and I wanted to do something my father would approve of."

"Uh, by marrying Jesep?" Presley asked.

"I did. I had failed my parents in so many ways. I thought I could do something to make him, well, not look at me as if he was sorry I was his daughter."

"You failed your parents by having me," Presley murmured. Billie didn't hear any hurt, but she knew it was there. Abandonment and rejection could cause plenty of childhood scars.

"I, uh, acted out a lot," Victoria said. "The pregnancy was just one of the things that disappointed them. And you weren't to blame," she quickly pointed out.

Presley made a sound as if he couldn't quite buy that, and he doled out some more questions. "Tell me about my bio-father. Is he connected to any of this?"

Victoria was shaking her head before he even finished speaking, but she didn't get a chance to add a verbal answer because of the loud voices in the hall. Or rather one loud voice anyway.

Ari.

"I will see Victoria now," Ari snarled.

"Let him in," Victoria insisted. "I don't want an altercation."

Billie couldn't rule out the possibility of their being one. Angel wasn't the sort to take crap from anyone, and Ari sounded as if he was on the verge of picking a fight.

Presley went to the door, opened it, and nodded to Angel, who stepped aside so Ari could rush in. But he wasn't alone. Olivia was right on her brother's heels.

Ari didn't seem surprised to see Presley or her in his stepmother's room. In fact, Billie got the distinct impression that he'd not only known they were there, but it was the reason he'd been so adamant about seeing Victoria.

"What the hell is going on here?" Ari demanded, directing that at Victoria. "Why are you talking to them?"

"They saved my life," Victoria said, which, of course, wasn't an answer that placated a clearly riled Ari.

Olivia wasn't in the anger mode, but she did seem confused at her brother's reaction. She tried to take hold of Ari's arm, but he threw off her grip with far more force than required. It caused Olivia to stagger back, and she might have fallen against the wall if Presley hadn't reached out and steadied her. She muttered a thanks that got lost in her brother's words.

"Are you working together with them?" Ari snapped. "Is that why they're here? You need to tie up some loose ends from your fake kidnapping?"

Victoria's forehead bunched up, and she seemed confused. Welcome to the club. Billie was experiencing the same thing. Apparently, Presley, too, judging from the question he hurled at Ari.

"Why the hell would you think the kidnapping was fake?" Presley aimed a glare at Ari.

"Sympathy, for one," Ari fired back. "So that Olivia and I won't hate her for Dad's will. Well, we do hate her, and faking her abduction won't change that one bit."

"Sounds as if you should hate your father since it's his will," Presley argued.

Ari smirked. "Who do you think talked him into doing that?" He pointed to Victoria. "She somehow convinced him to leave her everything."

"I didn't," Victoria spoke up. "And I didn't fake my kidnapping." She held up her bandaged hand to remind him of what the kidnappers had done to her.

That didn't ease his smirk one bit. "A small price to pay to hang onto your husband."

Anger flashed through Victoria's eyes, and Billie was glad to see it. So, the woman had a spine after all. "I don't need to feign a kidnapping to do that," she said through clenched teeth.

"Oh, yeah?" Ari challenged. "What happens when Dad finds out about him?" He hiked his thumb in Presley's direction.

That drained the courage from Victoria's face. Not from Presley's though. He moved directly in front of Ari.

"Explain that," Presley said, his voice low and dangerous. It wasn't a request but an order.

Ari did take a step back, but he didn't tone

down his expression much. "I know you're her kid," the man said.

Oh, shit.

And Billie muttered a few more words of profanity.

Apparently, Olivia was experiencing a whole lot of surprise, too, because she gasped, and she volleyed stunned glances at Victoria and Presley. "Is it true?" she asked her stepmother.

Ari spoke before Victoria could. "Yes, it's true. Victoria got knocked up when she was a teenager, had him, and tried to hide her secret by giving him away. Well, secrets don't always stay hidden."

"How did you find out?" Billie asked just as Olivia said, "Does Dad know?" The shock was still straining her voice.

Again, it was Ari who answered. "No. I was going to tell him, but before I could do that, Victoria was kidnapped. Convenient, huh? And convenient, too, that the kidnappers requested her son to do the ransom drop."

"It wasn't convenient," Victoria murmured. "It was a nightmare, and I didn't arrange it because you were going to tell Jesep about the child I had. I had no idea you knew. How did you know?" she pressed, paraphrasing Billie's earlier question.

"I have my ways," he said. The smug SOB. He was practically gloating now over Victoria's obvious distress. "Like I said, secrets don't stay secret. Do they?" he asked, not directing that at Victoria or Presley.

But at Olivia.

"No," Victoria blurted, and she would have bolted from the bed had Billie not rushed to her to keep her in place. "No," she repeated, frantically shaking her head. "Please, Ari. Not like this. *Please*."

What the heck?

Billie looked at Presley to see if he knew what this was about, but he didn't. In fact, the only two people in the room who seemed to know what was going on was the gloating Ari and the terrified Victoria.

"Please, don't," Victoria repeated on a sob.

But Ari ignored her and turned to Olivia. "Victoria got knocked up when she was a teenager, and she had him." He tipped his head to Presley. "And you. Twins. Sorry, little sister, but Victoria is the bitch who gave birth to you."

CHAPTER THIRTEEN

☆

Presley had to mentally replay Ari's words a couple of times before they sank in. And they didn't sink in well.

"Shit," he muttered, and he wanted to follow it with a string of bad profanity, but then he looked at Ari's face.

That arrogant sonofabitch was loving this. He was loving it as he watched Victoria and Olivia. They were speechless. Stunned. Gutted. Presley didn't want to give the asshole the satisfaction of seeing him that way, too, so Presley reined it all in, and he put on his cop's face.

"Get out, Ari," Presley told him.

Ari laughed and looked ready to spew more of his venom, but Victoria put a stop to that.

"Get. Out," Victoria snapped, and she sounded a lot stronger and significantly louder than she had just minutes earlier.

Ari lifted his chin. "Why should I?" he taunted.

Victoria looked him straight in the eyes.

"Because I control what happens to your father's estate, and I will cut you off at the knees. Not a penny. First chance I get, I will ruin you."

Ari certainly didn't laugh at that, but he still looked ready to challenge her. Then, he must have realized that he'd stepped in the shitstorm he'd started. He spat out some profanity, and without giving any of them a glance, Ari stormed out of the room.

"Is it true?" Olivia asked, and Presley saw the tears streaming down her face. "Is it true?" she repeated, her voice cracking over a sob.

Victoria nodded and seemed to take a moment, trying to compose herself. Presley was doing the same. Hell. This had been another gut punch.

"Yes," Victoria muttered. "It's true. I did give birth to Presley and you. I'm your biological mother."

"But..." And that was all Olivia managed to say for a couple of moments. "You can't be."

"I am," Victoria assured her. "And I'm deeply sorry you had to find out about it this way."

More silence. More tears. Presley was actually thankful that Victoria's attention was on Olivia because he needed the time to steady himself. The woman looked on the verge of completely losing it.

The woman, he silently repeated.

But she was more than that. She was his sister. *Hell.*

That required to take another deep breath, and he was glad when Billie moved closer to him and brushed her arm against his. Just that subtle contact helped him rein in the worst of the emotions, but it was going to take a while for him to process all of this.

"Does Dad know?" Olivia asked, and she pressed her trembling hands to her mouth while she waited for an answer.

"He knows," Victoria said, and she cleared her throat. "Jesep and my parents were friends, and when I got pregnant, Jesep told them that his wife always wanted a daughter, and they hadn't been able to conceive again after they had Ari. In fact, they were in the process of doing an adoption application."

Presley could see all of this playing out. Rich, snobby parents, their teenage daughter pregnant, and rather than try to raise their own grandchildren—or help Victoria raise them—they preferred to give the kids away. That way they didn't have to deal with the gossip.

Maybe her parents had thought they were giving Victoria a fresh start. A clean slate, so to speak. But obviously something had gone wrong for him to end where he had.

"So, your parents pressured you into handing over your child to Jesep and his wife," Presley finished when Victoria had been quiet again for several long moments. "Except it wasn't just one child."

Victoria made a sound of agreement. "When I got the ultrasound results and saw that I was carrying a boy and a girl, Jesep said he wanted the girl. He said he also had a close friend who wanted the boy." She stopped again, and a groan tore from her throat. "Jesep wouldn't tell me the name of his friend, insisting the couple wanted to keep the adoption private, but he swore to me they were good people and would love you as their own."

"Clearly, that didn't happen," Presley muttered. "So, something went wrong. What?"

She took a glass of water from the table next to her bed and drank several sips before she answered. "I needed a C-section for the delivery, and I ended up being fully sedated. After I woke up in recovery, my mother was there, and she said the babies were already with their parents."

Well, shit. That had to have knocked Victoria for a proverbial loop.

"My mother insisted that I was to put all of this behind me and never shame her or my father again. I didn't even get to see either of you," Victoria added with her voice outright shaking now. "You were just gone."

Presley wasn't immune to those tears in her eyes. Nor the ones in Olivia's eyes. But he needed answers.

"How did I end up in a fire station?" he came out and asked.

Victoria shook her head and drank more of the water. "I'm not sure. I didn't know you had been abandoned there until you told me right here in this hospital room. I just assumed Jesep's friends had adopted you as planned." She stopped, groaned." I need to ask Jesep about that," she added in a mutter, and her expression said she was dreading that conversation.

"Dad knew you had given birth to me," Olivia said in a hoarse whisper. "Mom knew."

"They did," Victoria verified.

"And they never said a word. They never told me…" Olivia seemed to freeze. "The bone marrow. That's why you and I were a match."

Victoria nodded. "When you got sick, Jesep contacted me and asked me to be tested. I did it, and I was a donor match. Jesep was…grateful," she said after seemingly searching for the right word.

"So, you married Jesep to be with your daughter?" Presley concluded.

"Yes. But he insisted I never tell Olivia the truth."

Presley recalled Victoria saying that Jesep had never wanted Ari and Olivia to think of Victoria as their mother. Ironic since she was Olivia's child and not Jesep's.

"Oh, God," Olivia blurted. "He knew. Dad knew. You knew," she said, looking at Victoria.

"We did, and I'm sorry we didn't tell you," Victoria insisted. "You had the right to know, especially after your mom died."

Olivia shook her head. Not a gentle motion. But a frantic denial. "I can't do this. I just can't." She said, throwing open the door and bolting out of the room.

Angel was right there, and Presley and he exchanged a glance before Angel set off after Olivia, no doubt to make sure she was all right.

"Ari," Victoria spat out. "He should have never done this."

"How did he know?" Presley asked.

Victoria opened her mouth but closed it. Her forehead bunched up before she whispered, "I have no idea."

"Would Jesep have told him?" Billie pressed.

"I wouldn't have thought so, but maybe Jesep said something when I was a hostage."

"Maybe," Presley agreed. "But I can't see Jesep mentioning me to Ari. Olivia, yes, but not me. That means Ari would have had to do some digging, and finding that kind of info takes time."

Victoria stared at him. "You believe Ari found out some other way. But how?"

"Don't know yet, but consider all of what's happened in the span of a couple of weeks. Jesep changes his will, cutting out Ari and Olivia and leaving everything to you. I doubt they'd be happy about that."

"They weren't," Victoria was quick to confirm. "Ari left in an angry tirade much as he did today."

"Don't doubt it," Presley commented. "He could have sulked for a while, but at some point, he might have started to consider how he could fix this. And maybe one fix was to kidnap, and kill, you."

Victoria moaned, but she didn't look that

surprised. He wondered though if she'd considered the rest of what might have been Ari's plan.

"Ari might have been worried about your bio-son having a claim to your estate, so that could have been why the kidnappers requested me. As Billie pointed out, she could have been added as a distraction, so that I might not be on top of my game."

The kidnappers had been wrong about that though. Billie hadn't been a distraction. She had only given Presley more reason to get Victoria, their fellow operatives, and her out of the attack alive.

He could practically hear Victoria trying to wrap her mind around all of that. "You believe Ari planned to have Olivia killed too?"

"Maybe," he settled for saying.

But there was a huge question mark there. Because if Ari hadn't honchoed the kidnapping, then the next logical suspect was Olivia.

Olivia had seemed genuinely shaken up over learning that Victoria was her mother and that Presley was her twin brother. It could have all been an act though. In fact, Olivia could have known about her bio-mom for years if she did any checking into the bone marrow transplant. Olivia could have kept it a secret.

Until her father's will.

Then, she could have set the plan into motion.

It twisted at him, but Presley knew he was going to do more than just consider that theory. He was going to have to look at Olivia as a person who wanted both Victoria and him dead.

"What about Jesep?" Billie asked. "Could he have arranged for you to be kidnapped?"

Victoria certainly didn't jump to deny that, and just considering it tightened all the muscles in her face. "I don't know. The will was a shock. I mean, it doesn't make sense. Jesep said he wanted Ari and Olivia to make their own fortunes like he did, but he bought his business with old family money."

Presley recalled reading that in one of the reports on Jesep, but he was having trouble coming up with a motive. He couldn't see Jesep wanting the publicity or the sympathy something like this would get him. Unless...

"Tell me about your will," Presley said. "Who inherits when you die?"

Victoria looked stunned for a couple of seconds. "Jesep, but I had it worded to include any child I might have, either biologically or adopted."

Bingo. That could be a powerful motive, especially since Victoria was just as wealthy as Jesep.

"So, we're back to square one," Billie said on a huff. "Ari, Jesep or Olivia could be behind the kidnapping. Or Hattie," she tacked onto that. "She's a woman involved in a case that Presley and I worked when we were cops."

"Four suspects," Victoria muttered. "And the three of us were probably meant to die at the creek." She didn't wait for Billie or him to respond.

"You need to talk to someone else. Someone who might be able to give us answers."

"Who?" Presley couldn't ask fast enough.

"Your biological father," Victoria said, eventually.

"But you said he wasn't part of this," he reminded her.

"He's not. Not directly, anyway." Victoria groaned, but she kept her gaze pinned to his. "His name is Joe Malloy. And he's the stepfather of the two men who kidnapped me."

———————— ☆ ————————

CHAPTER FOURTEEN

———— ☆ ————

Well, hell. Billie hadn't seen this coming. Apparently, neither had Presley because he seemed just as stunned as she was.

"I never met Craig and Ellis," Victoria added while they just stood there, staring at her. "And I didn't know they were my kidnappers until you mentioned them."

"You should have said something the moment you heard their names," Presley insisted.

"Yes, I should have. But Jesep was here, and I would have had to explain…everything. I'm sorry," the woman tacked onto that.

That apology sounded plenty genuine enough, but Billie wasn't going to dole out any *there, there* or *it's okay* assurances. Because it wasn't okay. This was a connection the cops should know about.

"Where's Joe now?" Presley asked. "And have you spoken to him about Craig and Ellis?"

"No," Victoria was quick to say. "I haven't seen or spoken to him in years, not since I married

Jesep. I have no idea where he is."

Billie did, and she took out her phone to access one of the reports she'd read about the death notification that SAPD had done. She located Joe's address and showed it to Presley.

"We can be there in fifteen minutes," Presley muttered.

"You're going to see him," Victoria said in a whisper, and she seemed on the verge of an objection or something. But she didn't voice it. She nodded. "Of course, you'd want to see him. He's your father."

"That's not why I want to see him," Presley assured her. "I need to find out if he had you kidnapped and if he's the one who tried to kill all of us."

"No," Victoria blurted, and she practically leapt from the bed. "He wouldn't. Not Joe."

"You haven't seen him in decades," Presley reminded her. "You have no idea what he's capable of."

"He wouldn't hurt me." There wasn't any doubt in her voice, but Presley didn't seem convinced.

"We'll soon find out," Presley said, motioning for Billie to follow him. "We'll let you know what he has to say."

They went out and found Angel there. "Where's Olivia?" Presley asked as Angel said, "What's wrong."

Angel responded first. "I caught up with Olivia in the parking lot, but she sped off. I let Ruby know so she can send someone to check on her."

"Thanks," Presley said, scrubbing his hand over his face. "I'll have a lot to catch you up on, but for now, Billie and I are going to see my bio-father. He's also the stepfather of our dead kidnappers."

The shock registered in Angel's eyes. "Fuck."

"Yeah," Presley agreed. "Keep me posted about Olivia," he added, and Billie and he headed out of the hospital and to the parking lot.

Billie plugged Joe's address into the GPS, and while Presley started the drive, she initiated a background check on the man. Presley used his Bluetooth to send a text to Ruby to let her know what was going on. Soon, Billie would have to give Owen an update, too, but for now she focused on Joe. Or rather that's what she started to do, and she saw the report that just popped into her inbox.

Oh, the irony.

"Olivia's DNA results are back," Billie let Presley know after he had finished his text. "She's your sister."

She stayed a moment to give him some time to absorb that. Of course, that wasn't something to be absorbed in a matter of minutes, but Presley nodded after only a couple of seconds.

"You're doing a run on Joe?" he asked.

Billie sighed, not because he was clearly diving back into work but because diving was their only option right now. They needed to know if there was still a threat to Victoria's and their lives.

"I am. Do you want to try to call him first and

see if he's home?" Billie asked.

Presley didn't hesitate. "No. I don't want to give him a heads-up. If he's not there, we'll track him down. Does he work in Bulverde, too?"

Billie thumbed through the background that had just loaded. "I think he works from home. He's a sculptor. A rather successful one."

She held up a photo of one of the man's pieces. A bronze of a woman on horseback. Then, she showed him one of the man himself. A lanky build with a thin face. Unlike Victoria's father, there wasn't a lot of resemblance between Presley and him except for their mouths.

Presley made a sound that could have meant anything. "Does he have a criminal record?"

"Nothing as an adult," Billie said. "There's a sealed juvie record though. He's fifty-two. Widower. He married Craig and Ellis' mom ten years ago, and she died just four years later."

"So, he didn't raise his stepsons," Presley concluded.

"No. Ellis would have been nineteen and Craig, twenty-one. Damon, a couple of years older than that."

She kept scouring the background, looking for any red flags. But she didn't see any. So, she went a step further.

"I'll put both his and Victoria's names in the data mining program," Billie explained, doing that as she spoke. "I'll see if they're linked in any kind of way."

Victoria had said she hadn't seen him in decades, but she could have been lying. Until a few minutes ago, Billie had trusted the woman to tell them the truth. That had changed though with Victoria withholding the very important tidbit about her kidnapper's father.

A text popped up on the dash screen. From Ruby. *Brief me, thoroughly, after you talk to Joe Malloy.*

Billie figured Ruby wasn't any happier about this latest development than they were, and soon, Presley would have to deal with getting hit with yet another personal bombshell. Twenty-four hours ago, he hadn't known who his bio parents were, and now they were front and center in this investigation.

On the prompt from the GPS, Presley took the turn toward Bulverde just as his phone rang. Not Ruby but a familiar name.

Olivia.

Presley answered it on speaker. "Where are you?' he asked, not exactly the tone of a brother. He was in the cop mode again.

"I'm driving around, debating what to do," Olivia answered. "Did you know she gave birth to us?"

"Not until a few hours ago," Presley answered. A muscle flickered in his jaw, and Billie thought he might be debating telling her the rest. The name of their bio-father.

"Is it true?" she pressed.

"Yes," he assured her.

Olivia didn't question how he'd gotten that verification, but Billie had no trouble hearing the woman's sob. It sounded real. And maybe it was. However, Billie wasn't taking anything at face value when it came to Victoria's stepkids.

Or Victoria herself.

Billie couldn't figure out a reason for the woman to orchestrate her own kidnapping, but maybe that's where Joe could help. Then again, the man might not spill the truth either. Heck, he might not even be willing to talk to them.

"What should I do?" Olivia asked. "What are you going to do?" she amended.

"To be determined. But you should go home. And avoid Jesep if you can," he tacked onto that.

"Dad," Olivia muttered, and she groaned. "All this time, he knew."

Yes, and Billie wondered just how much more Jesep had known. There was just something way off about this whole mess. Jesep's will. Him trying to keep his kids from thinking of Victoria as their mother.

Had any or all of that played into the kidnapping?

Again, it was a question with no answer.

"Go home," Presley repeated to Olivia. "I'll be in touch soon." With that, he ended the call as they reached the outskirts of Bulverde.

The GPS directed them not toward the center of town but to a neighborhood, Sterling Heights, that was more country than city with its large multi-acre, heavily treed lots.

"Yes, he's successful," Billie muttered, glancing at the large houses. Mansions, really.

Presley went to the address, pulling into the driveway of a hacienda-style house that sprawled in the center of the massive lot.

"You need a minute," Billie asked him.

But Presley waved that off, and he would have gotten out right then if she hadn't taken hold of his arm. Because she thought they could both use it, she leaned in and kissed him. She kept it short but not so sweet. After all, it was impossible to keep the heat out of even a kiss of comfort.

"Thanks," Presley said, giving her a quick kiss before they both got out of the SUV.

It occurred to her as they approached the gated area of the front courtyard that it could be locked and they might not even get to the front door. However, as they approached, the gate made a clicking sound and then swung open.

The front door opened, too.

And there was Joe Malloy, not looking one bit surprised to see them.

He was barefooted and had on well-worn jeans and a black tee. A man who looked comfortable not only in his clothes but his own skin.

"Victoria just texted me," he said, sweeping his gaze over Presley as if trying to take him all in. He wasn't smiling, not with his mouth anyway, but it was there in his eyes for a moment or two, until

Presley spoke.

"Victoria said she hadn't seen you in years," Presley snapped.

Joe lifted his shoulder and stepped to the side, motioning for them to come in. "She hadn't. Nor has she texted or called. She found my number on my webpage and let me know you were probably on your way to see me."

Presley didn't budge for a couple of seconds, but he finally huffed and went in. The house's interior was just as impressive as the outside, and she immediately saw some bronze pieces that she suspected were his work.

"This way," Joe said, leading them through the house. Two white cats darted out of one of the room, rubbing against his legs as he walked. He leaned down and gave them scratches behind their heads before they made it into a large kitchen.

"I've made both coffee and tea," Joe said, offering them a seat at the colorful tiled kitchen table. "And I debated making lemonade." He chuckled. "Nerves. I always hoped that one day I'd get to meet you. I'm sorry it's under these circumstances."

Presley didn't address any of that, and he continued to watch Joe with a cool stare. "Did your stepsons know about your relationship with Victoria?"

Joe seemed to shift gears, and sighing, he sat down in one of the chairs. "No. Even my wife didn't know. Victoria wanted it all kept secret, and I told no one. If I'd thought for one second that Ellis and Craig knew about Victoria, that they'd learned about you and your sister, I would have told the cops when they came out to tell me my stepsons were dead."

"You should have told them," Presley insisted.

Joe frowned, nodded. "Maybe. But it wasn't my secret to tell. It was Victoria's. I figured once she heard the names of the men who'd kidnapped her and if she recognized them, then she could have told the police."

Presley shook his head. "She didn't. And now possibly a very valuable thread of the kidnapping hasn't been investigated."

Joe folded his hands on the table and leaned in. "I can't believe Craig or Ellis found out that Victoria and I had children. It would have taken some serious hacking skills, which neither of them have. And why would they have even gone looking for something like that?"

Billie couldn't immediately think of a reason to assume their stepfather had had a relationship with an heiress.

"You're sure you never mentioned Victoria's name around your wife or them?" Billie asked.

"Positive. If they found out about Victoria and me, then they found it from someone else."

"Like who?" Presley was quick to ask.

Another headshake. "I don't know. Jesep, maybe. He could have told the wrong person and it maybe got back to Craig and Ellis."

Ari had certainly known about it. And he could have been the one to tell the pair.

"Do you believe your stepsons acted alone?" Billie pressed.

"I don't know," Joe repeated. "They were trouble magnets. Not leaders, and they always seemed to follow the wrong crowd. So, I guess it's possible they were working with someone." He paused, met her gaze head on. "You think Jesep put them up to this?"

"Why would Jesep do that?" Presley asked before she could.

"I'd imagine the usual reasons why a rich bastard wants to get rid of his wife. Money. Because a divorce would be too costly." He huffed. "I'm just guessing. I have no idea why, and I have a hard time imagining anyone wanting to hurt or kill Victoria."

Billie couldn't be sure, but she thought the man still had feelings for Victoria. Maybe even still loved her.

"Craig and Ellis had some serious weapons in their possession," Presley continued a moment later. "Any idea where they got them?"

"Possibly from Damon," Joe answered after a short pause. "He always had a thing for guns."

"Damon has ties to a militia," Presley told Billie before he shifted his attention back to Joe. "Do you know where Damon is?"

"No. I haven't seen him in at least two years. All three of them were always getting into trouble, and they've been known to sell drugs to make some cash. Maybe they made enough to buy guns to use in the kidnapping." He paused again. "The news reports said Victoria was hurt, perhaps even tortured. Is that true? Did those bastard do that to her?"

Yeah, definitely some love there.

"She was hurt," Presley settled for saying. "If you want any details, you should get them from her."

Joe waved that off. "If she's happy with Jesep, I don't want to mess any of that up for her. That was a condition for Jesep marrying her, you know."

"What?" Presley and she asked at the same time.

"That Victoria never contact me and never tell Olivia that she was her biological mother. Jesep made her sign papers. Sort a pre-nup. If she told Olivia or got in touch with me, Victoria would forfeit five million dollars, and he would immediately divorce her."

Well, hell. Billie hadn't been a fan of Jesep before this, but now she despised the man even more.

"If you know about me, does Olivia know, too?" Joe asked.

"She does," Presley confirmed. "And so does Ari."

Joe closed his eyes a moment and muttered some profanity.

"You know Ari?" Presley added.

"I know of him. Just because Victoria and I

haven't stayed in touch, it doesn't mean I haven't... checked on her. Never in person," he insisted. "But through social media and gossip. Ari's ruthless. A lot like his father."

Billie couldn't argue with that, and she nearly came out and asked if Joe believed Ari could have teamed up with his stepsons, but Presley spoke first.

"Victoria said when she gave birth that Jesep came and took Olivia. Who came and got me?"

"Jesep," he said without hesitation. "He took both of you." His face tightened, and she saw the anger flash through his eyes. "You were both so little that you fit into one baby carrier, and he left the hospital with you. Without the doctor's permission," he added. "I mean, Olivia and you were preemies. Four and a half pounds each. You should have stayed in the hospital at least a couple more days."

"You didn't try to stop him?" Presley asked.

Now, the shame came, overshadowing the anger. "I couldn't," Joe muttered. "I was a kid. Sixteen. And Jesep was friends with Victoria's father, who'd already threatened to kill me. I didn't stop Jesep because Markham said if I tried, he'd kill Victoria."

"Shit," Presley snapped, and he followed with a loud groan.

"Yes, I said that and worse many times that night. I stood there and watched that sonofabitch walk out with Victoria and my children, and there was nothing I could do about it." Joe paused and seemed to be fighting for his composure.

"Jesep didn't take me to a friend to be adopted," Presley stated. He was no doubt fighting for composure, too. "Someone ended up leaving me at a fire station."

The shock, followed by the outrage, flared over Joe's entire face. He opened his mouth, but nothing came out. He shoved away from the table, and, pressing both of his hands to the sides of his head, he let out a string of vicious profanity.

"I didn't know," he muttered. "I didn't know." He turned away from them, and it was well over a minute before he looked at them again. "A fire station?" Joe questioned. "Which one?"

Judging from his expression, it wasn't a question Presley had expected. "The one on Saddle Creek Road a couple of miles outside of San Antonio."

Joe cursed again, but this time it was a quiet murmur. "My father worked there. He was a fireman. And it's where Victoria and I met sometimes."

Sweet heaven. That didn't sound like a coincidence to Billie.

"Did Jesep know your father worked there?" Presley asked.

"Maybe, but even if he did, he wouldn't have left a note for my dad, saying here's your grandson."

No, he wouldn't have because that would have

gotten Joe's father asking questions. Why had Jesep done it then? Had it been some kind of warped act of goodwill, leaving Presley in the hands of kin? Or had the fire station merely been a convenient location because it hadn't been in the heart of the city?

"Jesep," Joe spat out like profanity. "Why the hell couldn't Ellis and Craig have kidnapped that asshole? Why not him instead of Victoria?"

"Good questions," Presley remarked. There was a cool edge to his tone, but Billie figured it was masking a whole lot of anger and shock. "Maybe because Ari and Jesep were calling the shots?" He paused. "But there's someone else. A woman named Hattie Sinclair. She could have had Victoria taken to punish Billie and me."

"Hattie's sister was killed on our watch when we were cops," Billie supplied.

Joe stared at them for a long time. "So, it might not be Jesep or Ari."

"It might not be," Presley confirmed. "That's why we're here. We need answers, and since Craig and Ellis are dead, we can't get those answers from them."

"And you think I can help?" Joe asked. "How?"

"We haven't been able to find out where your stepsons held Victoria," Presley explained. "If we know the location, we can search it to see if they left any evidence behind."

Joe was shaking his head before Presley even finished. "I have no idea where they'd hold her.

Neither of them own any property that I know of."

"How about property you or another family member owns?" Billie pressed. "Some place private where they wouldn't easily be seen or detected?"

He was still shaking his head but then stopped. Cursed. "The Saddle Creek Road fire station," Joe muttered.

"What about it?" Presley asked.

"I own it. It's no longer a fire station, but I bought it about a couple of years ago with plans to turn it into a work studio. My father loved that place, and I didn't want to see it torn down."

Bingo.

Presley and she stood. "When's the last time you were there?" Presley asked.

"Months," Joe said on a rise of breath. "You really think they could have taken Victoria there?"

"We need to find out," Presley said.

Joe gave a shaky nod and went across the room to one of the kitchen drawers. He pulled out a key and handed it to Presley.

"Thanks," Presley said. "Is there a security system?"

"No. It's been broken into a couple of times over the years, but there's nothing to steal. There's nothing inside it."

Billie was hoping otherwise. Obviously, so was Presley because he was already heading for the door, and she was right behind him.

———— ☆ ————

CHAPTER FIFTEEN

———— ☆ ————

Once again, Presley found himself having to shove away thoughts. Of Victoria. Of Olivia.

And now Joe.

His biological family. But he couldn't think of any of that now. Couldn't even try to imagine how they might fit into his future. For now, he just had to focus on finding out if Craig and Ellis had had an accomplice. A boss. Because if they did, then Victoria, Billie, and he could still be in the path of a killer.

"I won't ask if you're okay," Billie muttered as they drove out of Joe's neighborhood.

"Good." Because he wasn't.

Maybe it wasn't the kidnappers' plan for him to go to the fire station. It was possible he'd never been expected to consider it as a holding place for Victoria. But Ellis and Craig sure as hell had sent him to his childhood home. An emotional twist of a proverbial knife.

So, it was possible this location was meant to

do the same thing.

Which led him back to Jesep or Ari.

Jesep, especially since he had personal knowledge of the fire station.

That reminder caused Presley to curse. "Jesep is the one who dumped me," Presley muttered. "I'll confront him about that, eventually. Maybe I can do that if he's arrested."

"You're liking Jesep for the kidnapping," Billie commented, and it wasn't a question.

"I am. I just don't know if that's because he's actually guilty or if it's because I want him to be."

"It could be both." Then, she paused. "But if Jesep intended to eliminate Victoria and any of her children, he'd have to go after Olivia, too."

Yeah, Presley had already considered that. "Jesep might have believed Olivia would never learn about Victoria being her mother. No knowledge of it, no claim on Victoria's vast estate. So, Jesep would inherit everything."

"True. But that doesn't let Ari off the hook. He could benefit from a wealthy stepmother, and you, dying if he thought he'd somehow get his hands on Victoria's money."

Yes, he could benefit indirectly since he would likely inherit it when his father passed away.

Presley considered that while he continued the drive to Saddle Creek Road. He didn't need the GPS for this particular destination since he'd come here several times. In fact, he'd driven here on his sixteenth birthday. He'd had a junker car back then, and he'd come to see the place for the first time. Since then, Presley had made two other trips.

Why, he didn't know.

There'd been no answers there. And maybe there still weren't. This could be an emotional wringer of a wild goose chase.

"When and how did you find out you'd been left at the fire station?" Billie asked, her question breaking the silence.

He didn't have to thumb back through his memory to answer that. "I was eight, and I heard my mom tell one of her friends. I asked her about it, and she confirmed it. Well, confirmed it in a way by saying that someone left me there so she could become my mother."

Of course, that was better than telling a kid he'd been dumped there by an asshole prick who had lied to his birth mother about where he was taking him.

"A few years later, I found the news article about it online," Presley went on. "Baby boy abandoned at Saddle Creek Fire Station. The date matched my birth, so I figured that was the place."

He threaded his way through several turns, passing subdivisions that had seen their better days. Thirty-six years ago, this had been more of a middle-class community with several thriving businesses, but when those businesses had failed, so had the community, and the fire station had finally been shut down about eight years ago.

There was a dinging sound to indicate an

incoming text, and Angel's name appeared on the screen.

Sheriff Bonetti located Damon Dumfries. He's scheduled him for an interview.

"Good," Presley said, dictating his reply. "Any initial indications he was involved with the kidnapping or supplying his brothers with the weapons?"

Not yet, Angel answered. *But they say a picture's worth a thousand words.*

An attachment loaded. A photo of a heavily muscled man in his mid-thirties. He was wearing dark camos and had assault rifles in each hand. There was a Bowie knife on his utility belt and a crossbow hooked over his arm. He looked more than ready to carry out an assortment of felonies.

I'll let you know if Bonetti can pin anything on him, Angel added.

Presley fired off another *Good* text reply and made the final turn toward their destination. He spotted the station just ahead, and he glanced around, trying to see the place through the kidnappers' eyes.

It was an ideal spot to hold a hostage.

The nearest neighborhood was surrounded by high privacy fences, and what had once been a strip mall across the street was now a self-serve storage facility. No one would have been around to notice a vehicle coming and going.

He pulled into the wide driveway and saw that the place was pretty much the same as it was years ago. All the doors were intact. The main difference was that the windows had all been fitted with full exterior shutters, not a slapped together job either. They looked as if they'd withstand a break-in attempt from curious teenagers, maybe not from someone determined though.

Someone with a hostage in tow.

Presley got out, doing a visual sweep of the area. No one was around, and he didn't spot any security cameras, not on the building itself nor across the street at the storage facility.

He moved closer to the station, testing the large garage door where the fire engine would have been housed. Locked. So was the front door, but before he used the key to get inside, Billie and he checked the rear of the property that backed up against several vacant lots dotted with mature trees. There'd be total privacy here to load and unload Victoria.

And he saw proof that it might have happened.

There appeared to be fresh tire tracks coming from the left side of the building.

"You want me to call it in?" Billie asked.

"Yeah. Best to get a CSI team out here to compare these tracks to the ones that'd been found on a trail near the creek." So far though, the vehicle itself hadn't been located.

They kept moving while Billie made the call to Detective Seth Martinez, one of the officers who'd been in Ruby's office at the onset of this ordeal. This area might be out of SAPD's jurisdiction, but

Martinez should be able to get that sorted out.

Presley tested the back door. Locked as well. There were a trio of windows here, all shuddered so he couldn't even get a glimpse inside. Too bad since he wanted a look around.

"Martinez will have someone out here in about an hour," Billie relayed after she'd finished her call. "They're short-staffed as usual."

He groaned. That felt like an eternity.

"Martinez did ask if we'd seen anything other than the tracks?" she tacked onto that.

"Not yet," Presley muttered, moving to the door and slipping the key into the lock.

He heard an odd sound, not the click of the key, but a slight movement as if something had shifted a little on the interior of the door.

"What's wrong?" Billie asked, obviously noticing the change in his body language.

Presley didn't answer. He lunged at her, hooking his arm around her waist. "Run," he shouted.

They did. But they only made it a few steps before a blast ripped through the door.

CHAPTER SIXTEEN

---- ☆ ----

Billie felt herself being hurled through the air, and she landed hard on the ground, the impact robbing her of every shred of her breath. And then the pain came just as it had when a bullet had rammed into her vest.

Presley moved on top of her. Sheltering her, she realized, since there was debris flying from... some kind of blast. Then, she recalled that look on Presley's face when he'd put the key in the lock. She hadn't heard anything, but he clearly had, and his fast thinking had likely saved their lives.

Billie shifted a little, just enough so she could look back at the door. It wasn't there. It'd been blown to bits. So had the frame and the shudder on the window right next to it. There were now gaping holes in the fire station, and thick smoke was billowing out.

"Plastic explosives," Presley muttered, and somehow he got up and hauled her to her feet. "We need to get out of here in case there are more."

Billie cursed since she hadn't even thought of that, but he was right. And this was almost certainly something the kidnappers had left behind. Maybe to be certain any potential evidence was destroyed, but maybe they'd known Presley and she would follow the trail of information breadcrumbs to here.

Where they could die.

With the return of her breath, she got a surge of much needed adrenaline. Presley obviously did, too, because they were able to sprint back to the SUV. Thankfully, nothing seemed to be broken or sprained in her body, but she figured she'd have yet more bruises.

They got inside the SUV, fast, and sped away while he gave the voice command to call Ruby. His boss answered on the first ring.

"Long story short," he immediately said, skipping the greeting. "I met with my bio-father, Joe Malloy, and he's the owner of the old fire station where I was abandoned as a newborn. He gave us a key, and when Billie and I came here to check it out, the back door blew up."

Ruby muttered something that Billie didn't catch. "Are you both all right?"

Presley looked at her, no doubt assessing that, and Billie nodded. Though *all right* was a relative term. They were alive, but, man, she was shaken to the core. Added to that, their clothes were smeared with dirt, grass stains, and ashy like debris from the explosion. Some of that dirt was on Presley's face. A glance in the mirror confirmed it was the same for her. With the bruises from the ordeal at the creek, they looked as if they'd both had their butts kicked.

"No serious injuries," Presley said, "but now I need to do some mop up and get the fire department and bomb squad out here—"

"I'll take care of mop up," Ruby insisted. "Just get out of there now."

She ended the call, and with the conversation over, Billie could hear her own gusting breath. She tried to rein that in so she wouldn't hyperventilate. Thankfully, Presley had already done the reining in. He seemed super focused.

And pissed.

"You don't think your bio-father set that explosive," she said.

"No." There was zero hesitation. "I don't think he's in on this. So, either Ellis and Craig left it as a way of making sure to destroy any potential evidence or their boss did."

That was what she believed as well. She hadn't gotten any sense whatsoever that Joe had wanted to harm either Victoria or Presley.

"My place is closer than yours," he said. "Any objections to going there?"

This time, she was the one who didn't hesitate. "None."

They'd have to give their statements to the cops, of course, but that would have to wait anyway until the scene had been secured. It was possible the entire area would have to be evacuated so the grounds could be checked for explosives as well. Then after that, the CSIs would be brought in, and hopefully they would find something, anything, to make sense of all of this.

As Presley drove to his house, his phone dinged with not one text but two, and since they appeared on the dash monitor, Billie could see the first was from Angel and the second from Ruby.

Victoria's being released from the hospital, Angel messaged. *Can't convince her to go to a hotel or to friends, so I'll be going with her to her estate.*

"Hell," Presley muttered.

And Billie didn't have to ask why he was upset. Jesep would be there. Possibly Ari and Olivia, too, and since none of them had been cleared from involvement in the kidnapping, it would be like the woman walking straight into the lion's den.

"Angel won't let anything happen to Victoria," Billie said. At least, he would try to make sure nothing happened anyway.

Billie moved on to the second text. *Mop up in progress*, Ruby informed them. *Stay put until you hear from me. Am forwarding a report you should read.*

Within seconds, there was another dinging notification, and the report loaded. "It's from the crime lab," Billie commented, and she began to scroll through it. "Holy crap."

"What?" Presley asked, keeping his attention on the curvy road.

"The lab analyzed the recordings of the phone calls from the kidnappers to Ruby and us, and they cleaned them up enough to detect and analyze some background noise." She looked at him. "It's Hattie's voice in the background."

It wasn't surprise that flashed through his eyes but more of that anger. "They're arresting her," he stated. Not a question.

"Yes, SAPD is heading out to do that now." She paused, continued to read. And her heart and her hopes dropped. "The lab says they can't tell if the voice is live or a recording."

"Shit," Presley grumbled. "Her lawyer will use that as a way for her to worm her way out of it." He paused, cursed some more. "And she could actually be innocent."

Billie had to make a reluctant sound of agreement. She wanted all of this to end. She wanted some hard justice to be served to the person or persons responsible. But she also didn't want an innocent woman being charged so the real perp could walk free.

She could feel Presley continue to stew as he drove, and Billie knew it was being fueled by what was left of the adrenaline and the hellish crap he'd had to deal with since he'd gotten news of the kidnapping. In that short span of time, he'd learned the identities of his birth parents and had nearly been killed twice.

"I'm okay," he said, and that's when Billie realized he'd noticed her staring at him. "How about you?"

"Fine, other than..." She nearly spelled out all the unfinished business, all the unanswered questions. But Billie merely added a weary sigh. That about summed up their current situation.

Presley matched her sigh with one of his own as he threaded his way through the winding roads of the Texas Hill Country to his house. Even though they'd stayed the night here, she hadn't noticed much about the place as they'd driven in. Hard to observe the scenery when you could barely stay awake. But she did some observing now. It was secluded.

And beautiful.

The white stone and log cabin perched on one of the limestone bluffs that dotted the area. The house was positioned to capture some amazing views. A far cry from her place in the city.

Presley gave the voice command to open a garage where she saw another SUV, a motorcycle, and a van. No doubt work vehicles that he used for the various ops. She had a similar set of vehicles in her own garage.

Billie grabbed her go-bag, which thankfully still had one clean set of clothes left. A set she'd have to use since it was hard to find a spot on her current outfit that didn't have dirt and, heaven help her, squashed bugs on it.

"Shower," she muttered, heading in the direction of the guestroom.

"Same." Presley went toward his bedroom suite

that was just across the hall.

They stopped outside their respective doors, and their gazes connected and held for the first time since before the explosion. She saw exactly what she'd expected to see. A swirling mix of anger and frustration.

At first anyway.

That all changed in a blink, and they moved toward each other at the same time. He reached for her. She reached for him, their bodies meeting as his mouth came to hers for a scalding kiss that heated her from head to toe.

Billie forgot all about the dirty clothes. Forgot about the explosion. Heck, she forgot how to breathe and decided air was overrated. It couldn't hold a candle to Presley and his amazing mouth.

She didn't stay passive in the kiss. No. The need was already claiming her, driving her to make the kiss deeper. Hotter. So, that's what she did. She kissed and took. Then took some more, and she let him do the same to her.

In another blink, the urgency kicked up many notches, and the touching started. Not groping. Too many bruises for that, but at the moment Billie certainly wasn't feeling any pain, especially when Presley slid his hand beneath her top and touched her breasts.

She heard herself moan. Felt more of that hot pleasure. Felt a whole lot more of the urgency and need.

In the back of her mind, she did consider the

lousy timing of this. It was likely adrenaline sex in the making, but her body didn't care about the reason. It only cared about the outcome. And thankfully, Presley seemed hellbent on giving her the outcome that would lead to release from this pressure cooker heat.

Somehow, despite the kissing and touching, she managed to take off her holster. Presley did the same, and without their weapons, they came together. Body against body, and she moaned again when he pressed against her center.

The ache grew. Demanding. Needing. Shouting for her to do something about it *now, now, now.*

She did. Billie went after his shirt, pulling if off over his head so she could slide her hands and then her mouth over all those tight muscles. Mercy, the man was built, and if the need hadn't been calling the shots here, she would have taken a lot more time to savor every inch of him.

Later, she promised herself.

Later, when they'd burned off some of this heat.

Presley wasn't in the later mode yet though either. He dropped his hands to her waist, and kissing her, he slid them to the floor. In the same motion, he rid her of her top, and like her, he did more touching and kissing.

She heard him mutter a curse, and she cursed too when he lifted his head. Billie followed his gaze and saw what had snagged his attention. The bruise from the gunshot.

"It's okay," she managed to say through her gusting breath, and she pulled him back to her.

Their mouths met for another of those raging kisses before they began to grappled with their clothes. Again, speed seemed to matter here so there was some jockeying for position along with rolling around on the floor.

Billie got him out of his jeans. Then, his boxers. While he did the same to her jeans and panties.

"Finally," she muttered.

But Presley only cursed again and started to fumble through the clothes they'd just discarded. It was probably only a couple of seconds but it felt like an eternity before he pulled out a condom from his wallet.

He got the darn thing on but still didn't start sating this roaring need. Instead, he repositioned them with him sitting on the floor, his back anchored against the wall, and with her on his lap.

Then, he slipped inside her.

"Finally," she said again, and this time, the frustration was gone, and in its place was pure pleasure.

Planting his hands on her hips, he thrust deeper into her, starting the strokes that fueled the fire even more. The urgency and need took total control. And Billie was fine with that. She was riding this hot storm, letting it take her to the only place she wanted to go.

And Presley was right there with her.

She felt the climax roll through her, claiming

every inch of her body. Claiming her, and Presley gave her those final strokes to draw out every bit of the pleasure. When she was spent, when she could claim no more, Presley let himself go.

———— ☆ ————

CHAPTER SEVENTEEN

---- ☆ ----

While he mulled over the phone call he'd just had with Ruby, Presley slapped together some turkey and cheese sandwiches. That was about the full extent of his food prep skills, and he chowed down on one and some chips while he waited for Billie to finish getting cleaned up and come into the kitchen.

It'd been damn tempting not to hang around with her for her shower, but he'd needed his own shower and change of clothes. Plus, if he'd stayed, they would have likely ended up having a second round of sex, and he figured her bruised, battered body didn't need that.

He wasn't sure what he needed—other than the over the counter pain meds he'd just taken—but he was pretty sure thinking time had to be part of what was left of the afternoon. Eating time, too, since Billie and he hadn't managed lunch, and it was already past three PM.

There was a mixed bag of emotions going on

inside him. He was troubled by the things Ruby had told him, but he also still had a nice buzz from being with Billie. Now, there was a jolt of energy from the food that he'd clearly needed.

But there was also the head stuff.

The nonstop whirl of thoughts and information. Once this investigation was over, he'd obviously have some sorting out to do.

He looked up when he heard the footsteps and saw Billie walk in to the room. Or rather limp in anyway.

Hell.

He took out the bottle of ibuprofen and put it next to the sandwiches.

"Thanks," she muttered. "You've already taken some?"

He nodded and got her a glass of ice water. "I should have moved us to the bed..." But that was as far as the apology got before she leaned in and kissed him.

"The location was great," she murmured against his mouth. "Everything was great."

Presley hadn't realized just how much he'd needed to hear Billie say that. And he gave her a quick kiss before he pushed the plate with the sandwiches closer to her.

"Eat, take your meds, and I'll fill you in on my call with Ruby while you were in the shower," Presley instructed.

She downed two of the pills and sat on a stool at the counter to eat. "Is this about Hattie?" she asked. "Did they arrest her?"

So, he'd need to dole out some bad news first. Of course, there hadn't been any good news in Ruby's update.

"Hattie's not at the cabin, and she's not answering her phone," Presley explained. That could indicate she was guilty. Then again, with her hatred of cops, she could be just uncooperative and avoiding them. "There's an APB out for her."

"If she comes here, I'm guessing your security is good," she said.

"Damn good. No one will get near the place without a sensor going off." And he'd engage his full security system to expand to the perimeter of the house. "It would be a big mistake for Hattie to show up and take on two trained operatives," he added.

Billie nodded, ate some of the sandwich. "So, what else did Ruby tell you?"

Presley took a deep breath first. "The bomb squad found five other plastic explosive devices at the fire station. They were on all the windows and doors so no matter which one I'd tried to open, it would have blown up."

She stopped in mid-bite and muttered some profanity.

"Yeah, someone definitely didn't want the cops or us to take a look in that building," he spelled out. "But I wonder if it could have been more than that. I mean, if Joe had gone there, he likely would have been killed."

"And maybe that's what his stepsons wanted," she finished. "Joe probably didn't put them in his will, but this could have been their way of getting back at him while cleaning up the scene."

That was a good guess on both fronts, and Presley continued with his update. "Damon didn't show for his interview with Sheriff Bonetti, but Bonetti was able to confirm the man definitely could have supplied his brothers with the guns and the explosives."

Billie stayed quiet a moment. "Is Damon the boss who orchestrated the whole shebang?"

"Bonetti and Ruby don't think so. Damon's apparently a follower, not a leader." There was a sharp beeping sound that instantly put Presley on alert. "Someone's coming," he said just as his phone rang. "It's Angel," he relayed to her.

So, not Hattie or an intruder, but Presley had to wonder what this visit was about. It probably wasn't good news.

"What happened?" Presley asked the moment he answered the call on speaker. He figured Angel was about to say that Jesep had dismissed him as Victoria's bodyguard.

"I've got Victoria and Joe with me," Angel said. "They insisted on talking to Billie and you."

What the hell? Presley had a lot of questions, including how had Victoria and Joe ended up together, but he held off on asking anything and gave the command to disengage the security so that Angel could drive through, triggering the alarms and sensors.

"You trust them both, right?" Billie muttered, and he heard the concern in her voice.

Presley was feeling some concern as well, but he had to nod on this. Added to that, Angel would have searched them both for weapons before he'd even brought them here.

He went to the door to open it, and Presley got a serious gut punch of emotions at seeing Joe and Victoria step out of Angel's van. *His parents*. It was going to take a while for that to sink in.

Angel's gaze went straight to Presley, no doubt checking to see if he was all right with this. Since he was far from being at that *all right* stage, Presley only lifted his shoulder.

"Elvis, scan visitors for weapons," Presley instructed his AI program, and he heard the slight whirring sound of the infrared kicking in.

"Female and male one are unarmed. Male two has—"

"No need to list Angel's weapons," Presley told the AI app because he knew Angel would be armed to the hilt. He stepped back to let them in.

Victoria paused in the foyer, looking at him, and for a moment Presley thought she might hug him. She didn't though.

She was still way too pale, and her bruises were an even darker riot of color today, only emphasizing them even more. Her hand with the reattached finger was anchored in a splint with a bandage securing it, but she was cradling it with her uninjured hand.

"Thank you for seeing us," Victoria finally said, and she nodded a greeting to Billie.

"Victoria wanted to come," Angel was quick to volunteer, "and she asked me to pick up Joe along the way. Olivia is on her way here, too."

Presley did a whole lot of silent cursing. While he trusted Victoria and Joe, he couldn't say the same for his bio-sister. He'd be using the scan on her as well.

"Jesep and Ari don't know we're here," Victoria let them know. "At least I don't believe they do."

Presley was betting either Ari or Jesep had Victoria under surveillance so, yeah, they would likely be aware of where she was.

And who she was with.

How the devil would Jesep react to his wife being with her teenage lover, the father of her children? Presley figured Jesep wouldn't be pleased about that, especially since he'd never wanted Olivia's parentage to even come to light. Still, there was that sort of pre-nup so Jesep could use the mere fact that Victoria was with Joe to get a chunk of her estate.

And divorce her.

He didn't think Victoria would object to that now that Olivia knew the truth about being her biological mom. But Jesep almost certainly wouldn't make a divorce easy on her.

"Security, rearm full system," Presley instructed, motioning for them to follow Billie and him into the living room. "Anyone want anything to drink?" he asked, and all three declined.

"All right," Presley added. "Tell me why you're here."

And he truly hoped it wasn't so they could hash out their personal relationship with him. Presley wasn't ready to go there just yet.

"I overheard Jesep and Ari talking about an hour ago. The Marbury collection of diamonds is missing," Victoria blurted as she took a seat on the sofa.

"Shit," Presley spat out. "How the hell did that happen?"

Another headshake from Victoria. "I'm not sure. But they were in full panic mode when I left the estate with Angel. Apparently, the co-owners of the collection sent someone to verify the safety of the stones after they got an anonymous tip that the diamonds were missing. When Jesep had someone open the vault, the diamonds were indeed gone."

"Who has access to the safe?" Presley couldn't ask fast enough.

Victoria's forehead bunched up while she considered that. "Jesep, Ari, Olivia, and any of their PAs. The security staff, too. Oh, and the appraisers."

So, way too many people, which meant there was ample opportunity for someone to steal them. Well, ample opportunity for an inside job, that is.

Victoria glanced at Joe who took up the

explanation. "I'm part owner of the collection," Joe said. "And I got the anonymous tip."

Presley definitely hadn't seen that coming. "Why didn't that info about your ownership come to light earlier?"

"I'm not the primary owner," Joe spelled out. "There are a total of four owners, and I only have a six percent share." His gaze met Presley's. "And, yes, Jesep could have possibly known about that. Maybe Ari and Olivia, too."

Presley tried to focus in on what this might mean. Were the diamonds the reason that Victoria had been kidnapped? If they were missing because they'd been stolen, then maybe Jesep could claim the diamonds were given as ransom to save Victoria.

Billie turned to Presley. "You think the fake diamonds could be the real ones?" she whispered.

He couldn't imagine a mistake like that being made, but the look he gave Billie must have let her know it was possible.

"I'll get them from the SUV," Billie volunteered, heading in the direction of the door that led to the garage.

"Does Jesep know you're my bio-father?" Presley had to ask Joe while they waited for Billie to return.

Joe shrugged. "I didn't think so, but it's possible that Victoria's parents mentioned my name to him."

"Or Jesep could have done some digging to

find out," Victoria added. "He might have done that so he'd be aware of Olivia's DNA and medical background."

True, and if Jesep knew, so could Ari.

"This is the text I got," Joe took out his phone and handed it to Presley. "It came from an unknown number."

Check your diamonds 'cause they ain't there.

That was it, no other details.

"Ruby's trying to trace it," Angel informed him, "and she's reported all of this to SAPD."

"Jesep's not going to like that," Victoria remarked. "He'd want to handle this in-house."

"Yeah, I'll bet he'd like that," Presley grumbled. That way he could try to contain the bad press. "What happens in a situation like this? I'm assuming there's a security cam feed of anyone going in and out of the vault?"

Victoria nodded. "There is. Ari and Jesep were getting that from the security company when I sneaked out of the house." She paused, her bottom lip trembling a little before she steadied it. "I'm afraid of what Jesep might do."

Presley latched right onto that. "Are you worried for your safety?"

She took her time responding, which in a way was an answer in itself. "I'm worried who he'll blame for this."

Presley figured Jesep would point the finger at any and every one in order to take the heat off himself. Something like this could destroy the reputation of his company.

"I'm assuming the diamonds are insured?" Presley asked as Billie came back carrying the small pouch.

"They are for the full appraised value," Joe verified.

Billie opened the pouch, spilling out the contents onto the coffee table. The sunlight sparked off the stones, sending rainbow prisms around the room.

All five of them leaned in for a closer look, but Presley had no idea if these were fakes or the real deal. Before he could ask Joe his opinion, there was another of those sharp beeping sounds from the security system.

"Security, monitor on," Presley instructed.

The painting above the fireplace faded, and in its place was the feed from one of the cameras. Presley immediately spotted the silver Mercedes making its way toward his house.

"Olivia," Victoria muttered, getting to her feet. Presley both saw and heard the nerves in her voice and expression. "I haven't spoken to her since she learned I gave birth to her," she added under her breath.

So, this might turn into some kind of venting session. Presley couldn't blame Olivia for needing something like that. Once this investigation was over and done, he might vent as well. He would certainly need to try to come to terms with it anyway.

The Mercedes came to a stop, and Olivia immediately stepped out. She looked at the house, but then her attention shot in the direction of the road. So did the security camera when it obviously detected some motion there, and Presley soon saw another vehicle. A sleek red Porche.

"That's Ari's car," Victoria muttered.

The Porche was speeding, and it braked to a screeching stop directly behind Olivia's Mercedes. Ari bolted from the vehicle, his attention nailed to his sister.

"Where are the fuckin' diamonds?" Ari shouted, whipping up his hand. Not empty. He was holding a Glock. "What the hell have you done with them?"

And he aimed the gun directly at Olivia.

───── ☆ ─────

CHAPTER EIGHTEEN

---- ☆ ----

Billie heard Olivia shriek, and on the monitor, she watched as Olivia ducked down behind her still-opened car door. Unfortunately, the woman didn't get down nearly far enough since her head was visible through the window.

Ari had a clean shot if he wanted to take it.

And with the rage tightening every muscle in his face, he certainly seemed on the verge of pulling the trigger.

Cursing, Billie drew her gun. Presley did the same, and with both of them moving, he made it to the door a step ahead of her. Angel was right behind them with his own weapon drawn and ready.

"This could be a setup," Angel grumbled. "Olivia could be trying to lure you out so that Ari can shoot you."

That had already occurred to Billie. And Presley had apparently already gone there as well because he opened the door only a fraction. Since Billie wouldn't be able to personally see either Olivia or Ari from where she was standing, she continued to watch the monitor.

So did Joe and Victoria. They'd stood, their attention pinned to what was playing out in Presley's driveway.

"No," Victoria blurted, and she turned as if to run outside, but Joe slipped his arm around her to stop her.

"I can't let him hurt Olivia," Victoria insisted.

"It might not be Olivia he wants to hurt," Presley said from over his shoulder. "You could be the target."

With her eyes wide now, Victoria stopped struggling, and a hoarse sob clawed its way past her throat. "Stop him, Presley. Don't let him kill her."

Billie knew Presley would do everything to stop that from happening, but they weren't even sure what they were dealing with here.

"Put away your gun, Ari," Presley ordered. "Olivia, get down on the ground."

Neither obeyed.

Ari spared Presley an annoyed glance, but he kept his Glock aimed at Olivia—who stayed put. "She stole the diamonds," he snarled. "She probably has them on her right now."

Olivia frantically shook her head. "I didn't take them. I swear, I didn't."

"You did," he spat out. "I saw you on the security cam. You went into the vault and took them."

More of that frantic headshaking, and Olivia shot a pleading look at Presley. "Please help me. I did go into the vault because I got a text from an unknown number saying the diamonds weren't there. I wanted to check for myself, and they were missing."

Billie had no idea if the woman was telling the truth about the text or the diamonds, but one thing was obvious. Olivia was terrified. That was a reasonable response since the person she believed was her brother seemed more than ready to kill her.

"I can show you the text," Olivia added, fishing through her pocket to come up with a phone that she then waved in the air.

"Down on the ground now, Olivia," Presley insisted.

And this time the woman listened. Sort of. Olivia didn't actually drop to her belly, but she did scramble toward the front of her car, ducking down behind the hood.

"The diamonds were there yesterday," Ari went on, his voice increasing in both volume and rage. "And only two people went in the vault after I verified they were there. My father and Olivia. Since Dad wouldn't do this, that leaves my *dear, sweet sister.*"

That last part was definitely not a term of endearment. His voice dripped with venom.

"I didn't take them!" Olivia shouted, and she

made another of those shrieking sobs. She was crying now. Or else pretending to anyway. "I think Victoria did it. She must have altered the security feed or something."

Victoria made a slight gasp. "I didn't," she muttered. "I have no reason to steal those diamonds."

Billie didn't say it out loud, but the woman did have a possible motive. If Victoria blamed Ari and Jesep for her kidnapping, she might have wanted to get back at them like this. Still, Billie couldn't see that happening. If Victoria truly wanted revenge, there were likely easier ways to do it.

"Give me the diamonds now," Ari yelled, and he moved away from his car, making a beeline toward his sister.

"Ari, stand down," Presley snarled.

The man didn't listen. He just kept storming toward Olivia.

Presley muttered some profanity under his breath, stepped out onto the porch and fired a warning shot. Not at Ari but over the man's head.

That got a reaction all right from both Olivia and Ari. Olivia started screaming at the top of her lungs. Ari made a garbled sound of surprise, and his attention flew toward Presley. He moved to shift his gun, to take aim at Presley.

Billie groaned and stepped out onto the porch with Presley. So did Angel. And they all pointed their guns at Ari.

"The next time I fire, it won't be a warning

shot," Presley snapped.

Ari stood there, glaring at them. But what he didn't do was turn his Glock toward them. "Just give me the diamonds, and I'll leave my idiot sister for you. Oh, right. She's your idiot sister. My sympathies. My advice? Save yourself some future misery and put a bullet in her brain. In her bitch mother's brain, too."

"Ari," Victoria murmured, causing Presley, Angel, and Billie to all curse again.

That's because the woman was now in the doorway behind them. Even Joe wasn't able to hold her back this time.

"What?" Ari said, his voice taunting now. "You didn't realize just how much I fucking hated you. Well, you sure as hell know now."

Victoria groaned, and her breath began to come out in short bursts. "Did you have me kidnapped?"

Ari looked her straight in the eyes and smiled. The sick SOB actually smiled. "I'm not going to confess to something like that." His expression went back to a glare though, when he glanced in Olivia's direction. "Now, tell your bastard love brat to give me the diamonds, and you'll never have to see or hear from me again."

"I don't have the diamonds," Olivia sobbed out.

"Neither do I," Victoria insisted. "But I'll give you the money, the value of the diamonds. Just leave, and I'll transfer the six million to your account."

A burst of air left his mouth. A laugh but not from humor. "Money won't fix this, *Mommy Dearest*. Those diamonds can't be replaced. Without them, Wessington Diamonds goes under. No one will trust us again. We'll be ruined, and I'll lose my legacy. Olivia knows that, too, and it's why she took them."

"I don't want the family business ruined," Olivia insisted. "I don't want you ruined." She made another of those loud sobs. "I just want you to believe me. I didn't take the diamonds."

That clearly wasn't diffusing any of Ari's rage, and he seemed to be on the verge of shooting. If he did that, Presley would have to kill him. While that wouldn't be a huge loss as far as Billie was concerned, she didn't want Presley to have to add that to his list of nightmares.

"I have the diamonds," Joe called out. "Put down your gun, and I'll give them to you."

Billie wasn't sure whose profanity was the loudest, but she thought Presley won that particular prize. Joe stepped out onto the porch with them, and he held up the small bag that he must have snatched up from the coffee table. The bag with the fake stones.

Well, maybe they were fake.

At this point, Billie didn't know what the heck was going on.

"You took them?" Ari asked. What he didn't do was ask who Joe was. Was that because he already knew? Or had he known that Joe was one of the owners of the real stones?

"I found them," Joe said, and the man just wasn't a very good liar.

Ari's sneer conveyed he felt the same way. "Enough of this bullshit," he snapped. "I get the real diamonds now, or someone dies."

The last words had barely left his mouth when Billie heard the sound of a car. A rapidly approaching one, and from inside the house, she heard the now familiar sounds of the security system alerting them.

Ari turned in the direction of the vehicle, and he did something that surprised Billie. He lowered his gun.

"That's Jesep's car," Victoria let them know when the black Jaguar came into view.

Presley cursed and glanced back at Victoria. "Will it do any good for me to ask you to go back inside?"

She shook her head. "I'm not going to let you face him alone."

Spoken like a true mother, but Billie knew that Presley wouldn't appreciate the gesture. Nope. He would want her out of the line of fire, maybe literally. But both Joe and she stayed put.

Jesep parked about ten yards behind Ari's Porche, and the man took his time getting out. When he finally did, Jesep stayed right by his vehicle, glancing around as if trying to figure out what was happening.

"Ari thinks I stole the diamonds," Olivia said

on a wail, and she bolted out from her car toward Jesep.

It took her a couple of seconds to reach Jesep, and she threw herself into his arms. However, he didn't exactly return the embrace. He kept his attention on Ari.

"You believe Olivia took them?" Jesep asked his son.

"Yes," Ari confirmed without hesitation. Then, he tipped his head toward Joe. "But this clown says he has them."

Jesep looked at Joe then. And also at Victoria. Jesep didn't have to convey his disgust at seeing them side by side because that particular emotion was all over his face.

"That clown is your father," Jesep said, glancing at Olivia.

Olivia was already shaking her head when she turned in Joe's direction. "No," she insisted.

"Yes," Jesep verified. He took her by the shoulders and had her face him. "Did you steal the diamonds?"

"No," Olivia repeated, still volleying uncertain glances at Joe and Victoria.

Jesep seemed to study the woman a moment as if trying to figure out if she was lying before he finally nodded. "All right. Get in your car and go home. I'll deal with this when we're all back at the estate."

Ari huffed. "You're just going to let her leave?"

Jesep gave his son a look that could have frozen

the hottest level of hell. "Yes, and you'll leave, too. *Now*," he tacked onto that, and there was no mistaking that it was an order.

Ari gave another of those huffs, but he eventually started walking toward his Porche. Jesep went in the direction of his vehicle, too. Olivia stood there for a couple of moments, watching them walk away before she finally started to move toward her Mercedes. However, she didn't make it to her car.

Because the blast tore through the air.

———— ☆ ————

CHAPTER NINETEEN

———— ☆ ————

At the sound of the explosion, Presley had a déjà vu moment. Because that was the exact sound he'd heard when the door to the fire station had been blown off its hinges.

First there was the deafening noise followed by the sensation of being propelled backward. This time though, he didn't actually fall but instead was pushed against the front door.

Billie was right next to him, hitting hard against the reinforced steel frame. Angel, too, on the other side. Joe and Victoria staggered back into the foyer. Not for long though. Victoria bolted out, her attention fixed on what was left of Olivia's car. Most of the front end was now a fireball.

It was hard to see through the billowing, black smoke, but he spotted Olivia. She was on her knees, and she was seemingly in shock as she looked at her car. Ari was a few yards to her right.

But Jesep was nowhere in sight, though his car was still there.

It was possible he'd been knocked to the ground. Or even been killed if he hit something hard. But Presley didn't like that he didn't have eyes on one of their top suspects.

"I'll call it in," Angel said. "And get the fire department and bomb squad out here."

Yeah, because there could be other explosives just as there'd been at the fire station.

"Olivia!" Victoria shouted.

Victoria scrambled out of the foyer, and she bolted past Presley before he could stop her. Joe was right on her heels, calling out to Victoria as she was calling out for Olivia.

Presley had no choice but to go after them.

And he knew he wouldn't be doing this solo. Billie and Angel were right on his heels as he jumped down off the porch and into the yard. He took hold of Victoria, pulling her back from what was left of the Mercedes. It was rare for a gas tank to explode in a fire—there wasn't enough oxygen in the tank for that—but it could happen, and that's why he wanted Victoria away from it.

"Get back," Presley shouted to the others, still firing glances around, looking for Jesep.

Hell.

Still, no sign of him. Where was he?

"Olivia," Victoria called out again, but this time, Joe was able to hold her back from running to her daughter.

The blasted smoke prevented Presley from getting more than mere glimpses of Olivia and Ari.

Not enough for him to tell if they were genuinely stunned by what had just happened or if they'd expected it.

"Damon," Presley heard Joe say.

With his gun still gripped in his hand, Presley whirled around to see Joe. He wasn't looking at the flaming car but rather just way up the driveway by the road, where Presley saw the bulky man wearing a Kevlar vest duck out of sight behind a tree.

"I'm pretty sure that's my stepson, Damon," Joe said.

Presley immediately felt the hit of adrenaline. The fight or flight mode kicked in. And he was going to fight. Damon was one of the missing pieces of this deadly puzzle. A piece who likely had a boss right here, right now.

But which one?

And he couldn't even rule out Olivia from his suspects' pool.

Yes, it was her car that had just blown up, but judging from the location of the fire, the explosive device had been set in the front of the vehicle. From the looks of it, it'd caused a lot of damage to the engine. Not much to the rest of the car though. So, Olivia or a henchman that she'd hired could have planted it, knowing she would not only be unharmed but that she would now look like a victim rather than a potential killer.

"He's not alone," Billie murmured, and she pointed just to the right of the tree where Damon had disappeared.

Presley had to pick through the smoke again, but he finally saw the woman, and he had no trouble whatsoever recognizing her.

Hattie.

So, maybe Damon had arrived with his boss, and if so, Ari, Olivia, and Jesep might all be innocent. *Might.* But Presley wasn't willing to trust the three of them just yet.

"Everyone move away from the car," Presley shouted. "And stay down. Ari?" he called out when he could no longer see him.

The man didn't answer. However, there was a sound. And it was something Presley sure as hell hadn't wanted to hear.

A gunshot.

It cracked through the air and slammed into Ari's car.

That got everyone diving to the ground, including Angel, Billie, and him. They landed in the yard next to Victoria and Joe. Barely in the nick of time. Before more shots came. Then, even more. A barrage of gunfire that had to be coming from an assault rifle.

It was possible Damon and/or Hattie had put a stash of ammunition in those trees. Since they weren't on his land, that meant he didn't have security sensors there to monitor it.

"Local cops, fire department, and bomb squad are on the way," Angel said. "Their ETA is about twenty minutes. But I've alerted them that there's an active shooter in the area."

Which meant the responders wouldn't be able to get too close. Not near enough to help anyway, and Presley didn't care much for them being only yards from Olivia's car where there could be another explosive device.

Presley levered himself up enough to take aim and fire at the trees. The response was immediate. More gunfire. And a lot of it.

He looked back at his house. Getting inside was out of the question since Damon or Hattie would be able to shoot them. Still, he had to do something.

"I'll crawl to the side and then behind the house and try to sneak up on him," Presley insisted.

Billie immediately took hold of his arm. "And I'll go with you."

Presley had a debate with himself about that. Because he still couldn't see Jesep, and he had no idea what Olivia's or Ari's intentions were.

"I'll stay put and handle anything that comes up," Angel offered. "And I can give you some cover by firing into those trees."

Presley didn't doubt Angel's abilities, but he could essentially end up guarding five people. Or being right in the midst of a killer.

"I'll handle anything that comes up," Angel repeated, his gaze sliding to Victoria for a second. "I'll also get Ruby to send out a drone so we can pinpoint the location of these asshole shooters."

Presley nodded. Then, he gave a second nod to

Billie before they went into a commando crawl. Damon or Hattie must have seen them because some shots came their way, slamming into the ground right next to them. Angel helped with that by sending some rounds into the trees. That stopped the shooters enough for Billie and him to scramble for cover by the side of the house.

"Once we get to the backyard, we'll follow that line of oak trees," Presley let her know.

Since the trees were spaced about ten feet apart, it wouldn't give them complete cover, but it might be enough for them to make it to the wild shrubs and underbrush. After that, they would have to make their way inch by inch toward Damon and Hattie.

They ran to the back end of the house, dropping down again to crawl their way to the trees. Presley could still hear plenty of gunfire, both from the shooters by the trees and from Angel. He could also hear the slight dings of his security system alerting him that he was triggering the motion sensors. Presley turned that off since it was a distraction.

When they'd reached the line of oaks, Billie and he stood and began to thread their way from one to the other. No shots came their way, so that let him know Angel's diversion was working.

Either that or else Damon or Hattie was waiting for them to get closer so they could gun them down.

Presley had to push that possibility aside and

keep moving. He thought of that glimpse he'd gotten on Damon. Of the Kevlar vest. The man had come prepared so it was possible that he'd added other measures.

"Watch for explosives," Presley whispered to Billie.

She muttered some profanity and slowed her pace even more, no doubt checking the ground for each step they took. Presley was doing the same, and it slowed them down considerably.

They finally reached the last tree and had to get down on the ground again to go through the underbrush. Definitely not an easy journey with the branches of the shrubs jabbing at them.

With each step forward, the sound of the gunfire got louder, and Presley was able to pinpoint the shooter's location. It was directly ahead in the thickest part of that tree cluster.

Since Billie and he couldn't go straight toward it, they had to venture off to the side again. Coming at it from an angle where hopefully they wouldn't be seen. They were still a good fifteen yards away when Presley caught some movement from the corner of his eye.

Billie and he immediately dropped down, turning their guns in that direction.

And Hattie came running out from the trees.

Presley took aim at her, but he didn't pull the trigger.

"Does she have a gun?" Billie blurted. "I can't see a gun."

"Neither can I," Presley whispered.

"Help me," Hattie shouted.

She wasn't running toward Billie and him but rather in the direction of the house, and as she got closer, Presley could see that her hands had been duct-taped together in front of her.

Hell.

Hattie wasn't the boss. She was another victim. Well, maybe she was. He had to consider though that this could all be a ruse to draw out Billie and him.

"Help me," the woman shouted again.

There was some movement in the trees, and Presley adjusted his aim there. But no one came out. However, a bullet did.

Someone fired. And the shot slammed into Hattie. The woman shrieked in pain as she tumbled to the ground.

─────── ☆ ───────

CHAPTER TWENTY

---- ☆ ----

Billie's instinct was to run to Hattie and try to help her, but her training overrode that. She stayed put, first assessing the situation by pinning her attention on the movement that she'd seen in the trees.

Because that's where the shooter was.

He could be waiting for Presley or her to come out from cover so he could gun them down. But waiting wasn't going to help Hattie. No. Presley and she had to act now.

"Keep Damon or whoever the hell that is occupied," Presley insisted before Billie got the chance to say the same. "I'll get to Hattie."

Billie didn't try to stop him. And she tried not to think of the danger he was putting himself in. Instead, she immediately took aim and fired a shot into the trees. She didn't send out a stream of gunfire the way their attacker had. She didn't have enough ammo on her for that, but she could create enough of a distraction for Presley to get closer.

She hoped.

Pulling the trigger on a second bullet, she rolled to the side. Good thing, too, because the gunman returned fire, and a bullet slammed into the exact spot where she'd just been. So, the shooter had her in his line of sight.

Good.

That meant he wasn't focusing on Presley.

Billie repeated the process two more times of shoot, roll, re-aim. Angel was helping her with that, too. He continued to send the occasional shot into the trees, and that would hopefully distract the shooter enough so that Presley could do what he needed to do.

She lost sight of Presley, but she knew he'd be weaving his way through the underbrush to get to Hattie. Whether or not he would actually be able to help her was anyone's guess though, since she might bleed out before EMTs could get here.

Billie pulled the trigger again, rolled and waited for the shooter to return fire. And waited. But no shot came. She levered herself up just a little, trying to see if there was any other movement.

Nothing.

In the distance though, she could hear the welcome sound of sirens. How would the shooter react to that? Would he run? Or would he pull out all the stops to try and kill them? That could mean he might be trying to sneak up on Presley for an ambush attack.

With that thought flashing in her head, Billie started to move again. Fast. This time, toward Hattie and Presley.

Even though there was no gunfire now, it was hard for her to hear with her heartbeat crashing in her ears. Still, she tried to listen. Tried to watch for any signs of planted explosives.

"It's me," Billie whispered when she got close enough to Presley and Hattie.

Presley had his hand on the back of Hattie's right shoulder, applying pressure to the gunshot wound. She was definitely bleeding, but the location of the injury hopefully meant nothing vital had been hit and that Hattie could survive this.

"It wasn't supposed to be like this," Hattie said, her voice broken from the pain. Her breathing was labored, and the woman was trembling from either shock or fear. Maybe both.

"What wasn't?" Presley asked while he continued to fire glances all around them. Billie was doing the same.

"All of it," she blurted. "I was kidnapped. Forced here. That shouldn't have happened."

Presley and Billie exchanged a quick glance, and she saw the questions in his eyes. She had her own questions.

"Damon Dumfries kidnapped you?" Billie asked.

"Yes," Hattie said without hesitation. "He kidnapped me and brought me here so I could die.

So I could be set up for the murders. He's going to kill both of you and put the blame on me."

Damon might indeed try to do that, but Billie didn't intend to make it easy for him.

"He'll kill Olivia, too," Hattie muttered a heartbeat later. "I heard him say she had to die."

"Why?" Presley asked, but he didn't get an immediate answer because a shot came at them.

The bullet hit the ground not far from where they were. Too close. Angel was quick to respond. He sent out a stream of gunfire.

"Don't let him shoot me again," Hattie sobbed out. "Please stop him."

Angel was certainly trying to do that, and he was getting some kind of help from overhead. The drone had arrived and was flying over the trees now. It was sending out some laser lights that would hopefully make it much harder for Damon to see much of anything, including them.

"We're doing everything to stop him," Presley assured her, keeping watch of the trees.

His phone vibrated with a text, and she saw Angel's name on the screen. Billie also saw the drone feed that showed the shooter's specific location. The SOB was in the center of the trees, and the only way Presley or she would have a shot was to get closer.

"Stay with Hattie," Presley told her. "I'm going in after him."

Their gazes met for a split second, and a dozen things passed between them. The most important of those things was for him to be careful.

Billie nodded, and the second that Presley moved away, she put her own left hand on Hattie's wound to keep up the pressure. She kept her gun ready in case Damon bolted from the woods and came out after them.

Presley went into a commando crawl through the shrubs, and Billie prayed that would give him enough cover to make it all the way to those trees.

"It wasn't supposed to be like this," Hattie muttered, causing Billie to glance at the woman again. "No one was supposed to die. I just wanted you both punished. That's why I went to Jesep."

Both Billie's body and mind went completely still for a moment. "Jesep," she repeated. "What does he have to do with this?"

"Everything," Hattie said on a rush of breath. "I went to him to tell him about what I'd learned. About Victoria being Olivia's and Presley's mother, about Joe being their father."

"How did you find that out all of that?" Billie pressed while she kept an eye out for both Presley and Damon. At the moment she couldn't see either of them.

"I hired a PI, and I poked around in the bone marrow database." Hattie stopped, groaned, and began to cry. "I thought Jesep would use it to punish Presley somehow. I didn't think he'd have him, or me, killed."

Billie cursed under her breath. Jesep had unleashed all of this nightmare. He was the one responsible. But Billie didn't think Presley had been his motive.

Not his sole one, anyway.

No, there had to be a lot more to it than this. Victoria's kidnapping, the missing diamonds, the attempts to kill Presley and her had a lot more to do with something other than merely punishing Presley for Hattie's sister dying.

The sounds of the sirens got louder and louder, and while she couldn't lever herself up enough to see the blue lights, Billie figured the responders were nearby on the road. Waiting to get the all clear before they sent someone in to help Hattie.

Billie saw some movement in the trees, and she readjusted her gun, ready to fire. But then she had to immediately pivot back when she heard something behind her. She whirled around.

But it was too late.

There was a man belly down on the ground, and he had a gun pointed right at her.

CHAPTER TWENTY-ONE

☆

Presley snaked his way toward those trees. Toward the sonofabitch who'd been trying his damnest to kill them. Ironic that that SOB was the stepson of the man who'd fathered him.

And Presley doubted that was a coincidence.

Whoever had put this shitstorm together probably knew enough details to understand that Joe's stepsons might get a kick out of being hired to murder his bio-kid, Billie, Olivia, and anyone else who ended up being collateral damage. Hell, the plan could be to murder Joe and Victoria as well.

And that brought him back to Ari or Jesep. Heck, even Olivia.

One of them had to be behind this.

Once he'd taken care of Damon, Presley intended to get answers about that from Hattie. It was possible she didn't know who'd hired Damon, but she might have heard something that could help.

Overhead, Presley heard the whirring of the

drone. Heard the occasional gunfire exchange between Angel and the SOB, but the loudest of the sounds were coming from the sirens. Judging from the volume, there was a small army of people waiting to assist. Angel would be their point of contact for that, but for the EMTs to come in, Presley first needed to eliminate the threat.

He kept moving, eating up the space between the trees and him. And hoping he had enough cover to keep his ass hidden so he didn't get shot. He thought of Billie, and the image of her flashed through his head.

An image of her naked and in his arms.

While it was a damn fine memory, he had to shove that aside plenty fast. Too much of a distraction. But later, he'd need to talk to her, too. To tell her how he felt about her.

"Later," he muttered, and he kept moving.

After what seemed a couple of eternities, Presley reached the tree line, and he bolted behind one of the oaks.

And immediately got shot at.

Damn it, the bullet had come so close that Presley thought he could feel the heat coming off it as it whizzed past his head. Apparently, his ass hadn't stayed hidden nearly well enough.

He drew in his body, trying to put as much as possible behind the tree. And he waited.

A moment earlier, he'd been thankful for the sirens, but now he wished he could kill the sound so he could hear. Damon could be moving in on him right now, and he wouldn't know it.

Presley dragged in a deep breath and dived out from the tree toward another one. In the same motion, he took aim in the direction of where that last shot had come. He didn't fire because no one was there.

He hit the ground behind the second tree and came up ready to shoot or be shot. But neither happened.

Where the hell was Damon?

Since he didn't have a clue, Presley scrambled behind another tree, his gaze firing all around. Until he spotted someone.

But it sure as hell wasn't the someone that he'd been expecting. Definitely not Damon.

Jesep.

The man was leaning out from a tree, and he had a gun. A gun he was in the process of aiming at Presley. So, he was the one behind this.

Presley felt the surge of hotter than hell anger along with a fresh hit of ice-cold adrenaline. He didn't need either to put an end to this shit.

"You should be dead," Jesep snarled. He fired, his shot slamming into the tree. He cursed and re-aimed. "And those losers I hired to do the job obviously failed."

Presley didn't respond. Not verbally, anyway. Using the sound of Jesep's voice, he homed in on the man's specific location. And once he had Jesep pinpointed, he adjusted his aim. He pulled the trigger.

And his shot sure as hell didn't hit a tree.

It slammed into Jesep, blowing the gun out of the man's hand and taking off a piece of his finger in the process. Oh, the irony of that. Sweet, sweet irony.

Jesep howled in pain. Music to Presley's ears, and he hurried to snatch up Jesep's gun so he couldn't try to retrieve it. When Presley stooped down, he soon saw the small arsenal of weapons right behind the asshole.

"You should be dead," Jesep spat out again.

"Yeah, yeah," Presley responded, catching onto Jesep by the collar and dragging him away from the other weapons.

Once he had the bleeding, cursing man a safe distance from the guns, Presley reached in his pocket for the plastic zip ties he always carried. He'd barely gotten them on the man when he heard a new sound.

A bad one.

A scream.

And he thought that it'd come from Hattie.

Hell in a big assed handbasket.

Something was wrong, and he was betting that *something* was Damon. Since Damon wasn't here, that meant he could have gone after Billie and Hattie.

Presley didn't commando crawl this time. He broke into a full-out sprint, tearing out the trees and racing to get to Billie. He didn't see her, but he sure as heck spotted Damon.

And he had a gun.

Presley had no doubts that his gun was poised and ready to murder Billie and Hattie.

He pulled up, getting into a position to take Damon out, but there were more gunshots. His heart stopped. Just stopped.

"Billie," he shouted.

He started running again. He had to get to her. He had to save her. But Presley soon saw that wasn't necessary.

Billie had already done the saving.

She was on her knees, her gun aimed at Damon, and the man was now sporting some gunshot wounds to the chest.

Fatal ones.

Damon dropped like the dead weight that he was.

———— ☆ ————

CHAPTER TWENTY-TWO

———— ☆ ————

Billie sat on the floor at the back of Presley's living room and watched the aftermath of the dog and pony show play out. She much preferred it to the actual shitshow since here no one was trying to kill Presley and her.

Well, not trying to kill them with bullets or bombs anyway.

Ari was aiming some nasty looks at both Presley and her, but she doubted he was going to be stupid enough to try to avenge his father, what with two security operatives and a cop in the room.

And that was just inside.

Outside the house was another operative, a slew of cops, the bomb squad, EMTs, two ambulances, and last but certainly not least, Ruby Maverick herself.

Ruby had arrived shortly after the first responders and had taken over the mop-up. The woman and Presley were now outside, talking to Jesep and Hattie, who were both being loaded in ambulances.

Billie was thankful for any and all help from Ruby. She personally had the adrenaline crash from Hades going on in her body, and judging from Presley's body language, he did as well. Unfortunately, he had a more active part in cleaning up the aftermath than she did.

No sitting on the sidelines for Presley. A few minutes earlier, he'd gone outside to have a word with Ruby and Jesep. Before that though, he'd talked to the EMT who was examining Olivia for the bruises and possible concussion she'd gotten when her car had exploded. Presley had also talked to his bio parents, filling them in on what'd happened with Jesep and Damon. And before that, Presley had told Ari to sit down and shut the hell up when the idiot had started spewing about how his father had been framed.

Billie had applauded that, literally, causing Ari to give her more stink-eye.

She reciprocated. Stink-eye wasn't her specialty but she could dole it out when needed.

Like her, Angel was in the sit and watch mode, too, now that they'd given their initial statements to the cops. In fact, he was shoulder to shoulder with her on the floor. There were available chairs and room on the sofa, but they'd opted for this space to put some distance between Ari and them.

"I demand to see my father," Ari snarled.

Not his first request. More like his tenth. He'd been mostly ignored except for those barked shut-ups, one from Presley, one from the deputy trying to take his statement, and the other from Olivia, who was apparently as tired of her brother's crap as everyone else was.

"No way was my father involved in any of this," Ari ranted on, repeating his vent for the umpteenth time.

"I beg to differ," Ruby said, coming back into the room. Presley was right behind her, and he made his way to Billie, sinking down on the floor on the other side of her. "Jesep just made a full confession."

Billie released a full breath that she'd been holding for too long. She'd figured Jesep would lawyer up and drag this out in a court process that could take years to unravel. Apparently not. Then again, he had been caught red-handed trying to murder Presley.

"A confession?" Ari challenged.

"A confession," Presley verified.

Angel smiled. "Did you threaten to shoot his balls off or something?" he murmured to Presley.

"No. I'm not sure he has balls," Presley remarked. "I merely reminded him that he was probably safer behind bars than he was on the outside with three highly trained security operatives that he tried to have murdered."

Billie had to fight back a laugh. The timing for that would be totally inappropriate since only a half hour earlier, she'd killed a man and they'd been in the middle of a near-fatal attack. Still, he'd been a bad man, and if she hadn't shot Damon, then he would have killed Hattie and her. This way, Hattie would survive, and the woman had already made it clear she would testify against Jesep.

The bad blood between Hattie, Presley, and her wasn't completely wiped away. It might never be. However, Billie thought the woman's feelings had softened some. They might have failed to save her sister, but Presley and she had saved Hattie.

"Did my father really want me dead?" Olivia asked, drawing Billie's attention back to Ruby, who was staring down Ari—and winning.

"I'm sorry, but yes," Ruby verified. "He also planned on you taking the blame for the diamonds he stole. Then, he'd intended on Damon killing you. Hattie heard Jesep give that order while Damon was transporting her here."

Olivia made a whimpering sound and dropped down onto the sofa. Victoria immediately reached out, pulling Olivia into her arms, and while Olivia didn't return the embrace, she didn't fight it either.

Baby steps.

There would need to be a lot of those over the next weeks and months.

"Of course, Jesep wanted Hattie dead, too," Ruby went on, "since she's the one who came to Jesep with the info that Olivia and Presley were Victoria's biological children. But he only wanted her to die after she'd been set up for kidnapping

Victoria. Jesep had already gotten started on that by planting a recording of Hattie's voice in one of the calls from the kidnapper."

That might have worked, too, because of Hattie's connection to Presley and her. It could have looked as if the kidnapping was merely a way to draw them into a dangerous situation so they could be killed.

"Did Jesep happen to say anything about hiring Joe's stepsons to do his dirty work?" Angel asked Presley.

Presley nodded. "He did mention the two birds, one stone adage. I guess he figured it would crush Joe to learn the stepsons had murdered Victoria. And he would have learned that because while Jesep didn't admit it, he would have had plans to eliminate Craig, Ellis, and Damon."

"Definitely," Billie agreed. "No way would he want to leave three loose ends like that."

"None of this makes sense," Ari howled. But it seemed to make some sense because he groaned, and he pressed his hands to the sides of his head and squeezed hard.

"It does if you understand your father was flat-assed broke," Ruby spelled out. "Because of some bad investments Jesep made, Wessington Diamonds was within a month of going under."

"No," Ari insisted. But that was sinking in, too.

"Yes," Ruby insisted. "You would have lost everything. The business, your home, and certainly your reputation. So, Jesep arranged for

Victoria to be kidnapped, and she was supposed to die at the ransom drop at the creek." Ruby glanced at Presley. "So were you."

Billie filled in the blanks on the rest. With Victoria and Presley and Olivia dead, Jesep would inherit Victoria's estate. All of it. No pesky next of kin kids to stake a claim on it.

She could also understand why Jesep had wanted her in on the ransom drop. Along with her being a distraction to Presley, having the two of them would have added more suspicion to Hattie's guilt.

Billie mentally cringed as to how close Jesep had come to getting away with all of this.

"But he left everything to Victoria in his will," Ari argued. He seemed to catch onto that as a lifeline, a hope that his father wasn't the asshole killer that everyone else in the room knew him to be.

"He was hoping by doing his will that way, he wouldn't be implicated in any way in her death," Ruby explained. "And if he'd somehow died first, then Victoria would have gotten saddled with all his debt."

"And the diamonds?" Victoria asked. "Where are they?"

"Apparently, in a safe deposit box in San Antoino," Ruby supplied. "Someone from SAPD is on the way there now to retrieve them."

There it all was. The answers to this nightmare that Jesep had started. Had started because of money. Yes, he would be locked up for the rest of his life, but he'd left so much misery in his wake.

But he had left a bright spot, too.

She looked at Presley. "If Jesep hadn't insisted we be in on this ops…" She stopped, figuring that was best said at a different time.

Presley obviously didn't think so though because he leaned in and brushed a kiss on her mouth. He didn't stop there. He stood, taking her by the hand and pulling her to her feet.

"Excuse us a minute," Presley said to no one in particular.

He led her out of the living room, through the kitchen, and into the adjacent laundry room. Presley shut the door, putting his back against it to stop anyone from coming in. Then, he pulled her to him and kissed her.

Really kissed her.

It was foreplay on steroids, and Billie welcomed every bit of the scalding heat. It was a wonderful change to dodging bullets and shooting bad guys.

Presley didn't cut the kiss short. He went in deeper, notching up the heat even more. Making her need him. And it was truly need.

It was also love.

She didn't want to think about that now though. She wanted to get lost in this heat. Lost in him.

But that didn't happen.

Presley pulled back, meeting her eye to eye. "I

figure we've got five minutes tops before someone comes looking for us, so I'll make this quick."

She lifted an eyebrow. "Five minutes isn't enough time." Billie winked at him.

He smiled, kissed her. And then got a very serious expression on his incredible face.

"I'll bottom line this," he said. "I'm in love with you, and I want to keep seeing you. Keep kissing you."

Which he did.

A thorough, Presley kiss that clouded her mind and made her whole body flutter with anticipation of even more heat.

"I want to keep having sex with you," he added.

Another kiss.

Somehow, he made that one the best yet. Long, deep, and perfect. He eased back from her, met her gaze again.

"I want to keep being in your life," he went on. "Did you hear the part about me being in love with you?"

"I did," she assured him.

And she kissed him. Billie made it count, too. She would never be able to dole out the heat Presley did, but she gave it her best shot and was rewarded when she heard him make a low grumbling sound of pleasure.

"I'll bottom line this," Billie repeated when she broke the kiss but kept her mouth against his. Because, hey, he was faster to move back into a kiss that way. "I'm in love with you, too."

She felt his mouth stretch into a smile.

"Good," he murmured. And he repeated it a couple of times while he nipped her bottom lip with his teeth. "Once I get all these people out of my house, we're going to have some great sex."

"Agreed," she couldn't say fast enough.

Of course, they still had things to work out. Well, he did anyway with his bio-parents and sister. They'd have paperwork and interviews to do. A debriefing with their bosses. But for now, it was just this moment.

Just them.

Just Presley and her.

So, Billie claimed his mouth for a long, slow kiss.

———— ☆ ————

ABOUT THE HARD JUSTICE TEXAS SERIES:

The Maverick Ops team members are former military and cops who assist law enforcement in cold cases and hot investigations where lives are on the line. Their specialty is rescuing kidnapped victims, tracking down killers and protecting those in the path of danger. Maverick Ops is known for doing what it does best--delivering some hard justice.

ABOUT THE AUTHOR:

―――――― ★☆★ ――――――

Former Air Force Captain Delores Fossen is a USA Today, Amazon and Publisher's Weekly bestselling author of over 150 books. She's received the Booksellers Best Award for Best Romantic Suspense and the Romantic Times Reviewers Choice Award. In addition, she's had nearly a hundred short stories and articles published in national magazines. You can contact the author through her webpage at www.deloresfossen.com.

―――――― ★☆★ ――――――

HARD JUSTICE, TEXAS SERIES BOOKS BY DELORES FOSSEN:

Lone Star Rescue (book 1)

Lone Star Showdown (book 2)

Lone Star Payback (book 3)

Lone Star Protector (book 4)

Lone Star Witness (book 5)

Lone Star Target (book 6)

Lone Star Secrets (book 7)

Lone Star Hostage (book 8)

Lone Star Redemption (book 9)

―――― ★☆★ ――――

Visit deloresfossen.com for more titles and release dates. Also sign up for Delores' newsletter at https://www.deloresfossen.com/contactnewsletter.html

―――― ★☆★ ――――

OTHER BOOKS BY DELORES FOSSEN:

Appaloosa Pass Ranch
1 - Lone Wolf Lawman (Nov-2015)
2 - Taking Aim at the Sheriff (Dec-2015)
3 - Trouble with a Badge (Apr-2016)
4 - The Marshal's Justice (May-2016)
5 - Six-Gun Showdown (Aug-2016)
6 - Laying Down the Law (Sep-2016)

Blue River Ranch
1 - Always a Lawman (Dec-2017)
2 - Gunfire on the Ranch (Jan-2018)
3 - Lawman From Her Past (Mar-2018)
4 - Roughshod Justice (Apr-2018)

Coldwater, Texas
1 - Lone Star Christmas (Sep-2018)
1.5 - Lone Star Midnight (Jan-2019)
2 - Hot Texas Sunrise (Mar-2019)
2.5 - Texas at Dusk (Jun-2019)
3 - Sweet Summer Sunset (Jun-2019)
4 - A Coldwater Christmas (Sep-2019)

Cowboy Brothers in Arms
1 - Heart Like a Cowboy (Dec-2023)
2 - Always a Maverick (May-2024)
3 – Cowboying Up (working title) 2024

Five Alarm Babies
1 - Undercover Daddy (May-2007)
2 - Stork Alert // Whose Baby? (Aug-2007)
3 - The Christmas Clue (Nov-2007)
4 - Newborn Conspiracy (Feb-2008)
5 - The Horseman's Son // The Cowboy's Son (Mar-2008)

Last Ride, Texas

1 - Spring at Saddle Run (May-2021)
2 - Christmas at Colts Creek (Nov-2021)
3 - Summer at Stallion Ridge (Apr-2022)
3.5 - Second Chance at Silver Springs (Oct-2022)
4 - Mornings at River's End Ranch (Dec-2022)
4.5 - Breaking Rules at Nightfall Ranch (Feb-2023)
5 - A Texas Kind of Cowboy (Mar-2023)
6 - Twilight at Wild Springs (Jul-2023)

The Law in Lubbock County
1 - Sheriff in the Saddle (Jul-2022)
2 - Maverick Justice (Aug-2022)
3 - Lawman to the Core (Jan-2023)
4 - Spurred to Justice (Jan-2023)

The Lawmen of Silver Creek Ranch
1 - Grayson (Nov-2011)
2 - Dade (Dec-2011)
3 - Nate (Jan-2012)
4 - Kade (Jul-2012)
5 - Gage (Aug-2012)
6 - Mason (Sep-2012)
7 - Josh (Apr-2014)
8 - Sawyer (May-2014)

9 - Landon (Nov-2016)
10 - Holden (Mar-2017)
11 - Drury (Apr-2017)
12 - Lucas (May-2017)

The Lawmen of McCall Canyon
1 - Cowboy Above the Law (Aug-2018)
2 - Finger on the Trigger (Sep-2018)
3 - Lawman with a Cause (Jan-2019)
4 - Under The Cowboy's Protection (Feb-2019)

Lone Star Ridge
1 - Tangled Up in Texas (Feb-2020)
1.5 - That Night in Texas (May-2020)
2 - Chasing Trouble in Texas (Jun-2020)
2.5 - Hot Summer in Texas (Sep-2020)
3 - Wild Nights in Texas (Oct-2020)
3.5 - Whatever Happens in Texas (Jan-2021)
4 - Tempting in Texas (Feb-2021)
5 - Corralled in Texas (Mar-2022)

Longview Ridge Ranch
1 - Safety Breach (Dec-2019)

2 - A Threat to His Family (Jan-2020)
3 - Settling an Old Score (Aug-2020)
4 - His Brand of Justice (Sep-2020)

The Marshals of Maverick County
1 - The Marshal's Hostage (May-2013)
2 - One Night Standoff (Jun-2013)
3 - Outlaw Lawman (Jul-2013)
4 - Renegade Guardian (Nov-2013)
5 - Justice Is Coming (Dec-2013)
6 - Wanted (Jan-2014)

McCord Brothers
0.5 - What Happens on the Ranch (Jan-2016)
1 - Texas on My Mind (Feb-2016)
1.5 - Cowboy Trouble (May-2016)
2 - Lone Star Nights (Jun-2016)
2.5 - Cowboy Underneath It All (Aug-2016)
3 - Blame It on the Cowboy (Oct-2016)

Mercy Ridge Lawmen
1 - Her Child to Protect (May-2021)
2 - Safeguarding the Surrogate (Jul-2021)

3 - Targeting the Deputy (Dec-2021)
4 - Pursued by the Sheriff (Jan-2022)

Mustang Ridge
1 - Christmas Rescue at Mustang Ridge (Dec-2012)
2 - Standoff at Mustang Ridge (Jan-2013)

Silver Creek Lawmen: Second Generation
1 - Targeted in Silver Creek (Jul-2023)
2 - Maverick Detective Dad (Aug-2023)
3 - Last Seen in Silver Creek (Sep-2023)
4 - Marked For Revenge (Oct-2023)

Sweetwater Ranch
1 - Maverick Sheriff (Sep-2014)
2 - Cowboy Behind the Badge (Oct-2014)
3 - Rustling Up Trouble (Nov-2014)
4 - Kidnapping in Kendall County (Dec-2014)
5 - The Deputy's Redemption (Mar-2015)
6 - Reining in Justice (Apr-2015)
7 - Surrendering to the Sheriff (Jul-2015)
8 - A Lawman's Justice (Aug-2015)

Texas Maternity Hostages
1 - The Baby's Guardian (May-2010)
2 - Daddy Devastating (Jun-2010)
3 - The Mommy Mystery (Jul-2010)

Texas Maternity: Labor and Delivery
1 - Savior in the Saddle (Nov-2010)
2 - Wild Stallion (Dec-2010)
3 - The Texas Lawman's Last Stand (Jan-2011)

Texas Paternity
1 - Security Blanket (Oct-2008)
2 - Branded By The Sheriff (Jan-2009)
3 - Expecting Trouble (Feb-2009)
4 - Secret Delivery (Mar-2009)
5 - Christmas Guardian (Oct-2009)

A Wrangler's Creek Novel
1 - Those Texas Nights (Jan-2017)
2 - No Getting Over a Cowboy (Apr-2017)
3 - Branded as Trouble (Jul-2017)

4 - Lone Star Cowboy (Nov-2016)
5 - One Good Cowboy (Feb-2017)
6 - Just Like a Cowboy (May-2017)
7 - Texas-Sized Trouble (Jan-2018)
8 - Lone Star Blues (Apr-2018)
9 - The Last Rodeo (Jul-2018)
10 - Cowboy Dreaming (Dec-2017)
11 - Cowboy Heartbreaker (Mar-2018)
12 - Cowboy Blues (May-2018)

Daddy Corps
G.I. Cowboy (Apr-2011)

Ice Lake
Cold Heat (Jan-2012)

Kenner County Crime Unit
She's Positive (Jul-2009)

Men on a Mission
Marching Orders (Mar-2003)

Shivers
20 - His to Possess (Oct-2014)

The Silver Star of Texas

Trace Evidence In Tarrant County // For Justice and Love (Feb-2007)

Questioning The Heiress (Jul-2008)

Shotgun Sheriff (Feb-2010)

Top Secret Babies

Mommy Under Cover (Feb-2005)

Made in the USA
Coppell, TX
03 January 2025